A Note from Stephanie about
Being in College

I'm sick of people treating me like I'm a little kid! I know I'm only in middle school—but I'm much more mature than any of my friends!

My teachers, my principal, and even my own family are acting like I can't do anything for myself! The only place I feel like an adult is on D.J.'s college campus. That's because I met a really great guy there! His name is Eric. He's cute, he's smart, *and* he's the editor of the school paper. Eric thinks my ideas for the campus newspaper are great. And he wants me to be a writer on the newspaper staff. There's only one problem—Eric also thinks I'm a freshman at the college.

So I'm pretending that I am a freshman. Just for a little while. But I can't tell anyone in my family about it. Because they would completely flip out! And with my family, that's a lot of flipping!

Right now there are nine people and a dog living in our house—and for all I know, someone new could move in at any time. There's me, my big sister, D.J., my little sister, Michelle, and my dad, Danny. But that's just the beginning.

When my mom died, Dad needed help. So he asked his old college buddy, Joey Gladstone, and my Uncle Jesse to come live with us, to help take care of me and my sisters.

Back then, Uncle Jesse didn't know much about

taking care of three little girls. He was more into rock 'n' roll. Joey didn't know anything about kids, either—but it sure was funny watching him learn!

Having Uncle Jesse and Joey around was like having three dads instead of one! But then something even better happened—Uncle Jesse fell in love. He married Rebecca Donaldson, Dad's co-host on his TV show, *Wake Up, San Francisco*. Aunt Becky's so nice—she's more like a big sister than an aunt.

Next Uncle Jesse and Aunt Becky had twin baby boys. Their names are Nicky and Alex, and they are adorable!

I love being part of a big family. Still, things can get pretty crazy when you live in such a full house!

FULL HOUSE™: Stephanie novels

Phone Call from a Flamingo
The Boy-Oh-Boy Next Door
Twin Troubles
Hip Hop Till You Drop
Here Comes the Brand-New Me
The Secret's Out
Daddy's Not-So-Little Girl
P.S. Friends Forever
Getting Even with the Flamingoes
The Dude of My Dreams
Back-to-School Cool
Picture Me Famous
Two-for-One Christmas Fun
The Big Fix-up Mix-up
Ten Ways to Wreck a Date
Wish Upon a VCR
Doubles or Nothing
Sugar and Spice Advice
Never Trust a Flamingo
The Truth About Boys
Crazy About the Future
My Secret Secret Admirer
Blue Ribbon Christmas
The Story on Older Boys

Club Stephanie:

#1 Fun, Sun, and Flamingoes
#2 Fireworks and Flamingoes
#3 Flamingo Revenge

Available from MINSTREL Books

FULL HOUSE™
Stephanie

The Story on Older Boys

Laura O'Neil

A Parachute Book

Published by POCKET BOOKS
New York   London   Toronto   Sydney   Tokyo   Singapore

A MINSTREL PAPERBACK *Original*

 A Minstrel Book published by
POCKET BOOKS, a division of Simon & Schuster Inc.
1230 Avenue of the Americas, New York, NY 10020

A PARACHUTE PRESS BOOK

 Copyright © and ™ 1998 by Warner Bros.

FULL HOUSE, characters, names and all related indicia are trademarks of Warner Bros. © 1998.

ISBN: 0-671-00831-5

First Minstrel Books printing January 1998

10 9 8 7 6 5 4 3 2 1

A MINSTREL BOOK and colophon are registered trademarks of Simon & Schuster Inc.

Cover photo by Schultz Photography

Printed in the U.S.A.

The Story on Older Boys

CHAPTER

1

◆ ◀ ✦ ◆

"Stephanie Tanner, ace reporter, on the job," Stephanie said with a giggle.

She shut her gym locker and stepped closer to her best friend, Darcy Powell. She pretended to hold out a microphone. "Tell me, Ms. Powell," she said in her best TV-reporter voice. "Do you know anything about the Big Cleanup Week, which is taking place next week here at John Muir Middle School?"

"Well . . ." Darcy's dark eyes sparkled with laughter. She spoke into the imaginary microphone. "It's simply impossible to remember *all* the activities going on for the Big Cleanup Week, but I do know that the entire school is very excited about it."

"That's wonderful," Stephanie went on. Then she sighed and opened her hand, dropping the pretend microphone. "I wish I felt the same way."

Darcy's smile faded. She looked at Stephanie with surprise. "What do you mean?" she asked. "I thought you were looking forward to the Big Cleanup Week."

"I was," Stephanie said. She brushed aside a strand of her long blond hair. "Until the editor of *The Scribe* asked me to write an article about it."

"So?" Darcy said. "You love writing for the paper. What's the problem?"

"It's a dull assignment," Stephanie explained. "I mean, who wants to read about boring activities for cleaning up the school? No one," she went on, answering her own question.

The two girls left the locker room and headed into the gym together. "I'm sure you can find *something* to write about," Darcy said. "There's the project to repaint the gym, and Litter-Free School Day on Saturday. Plus, there's the assembly next Friday. That's the really exciting part," she reminded Stephanie with a grin. "You and Allie and I are going to perform our skit."

"I know," Stephanie said. She smiled as she thought about the skit that she and her friends had written. It was a total goof. "I am planning to include all that stuff in my article. But I still wish there were a few more fun things going on to make the article more interesting. Every time I start to write it, I feel like I'm trying to get kids excited about the doing the dishes!"

The other girls in their gym class began to stretch out. Stephanie, though, was still thinking about the Big Cleanup Week. She pointed to a sign that was taped to the window of the athletic offices. "MAKE JOHN MUIR MIDDLE SCHOOL MORE BEAUTIFUL. HELP RE-PAINT THE GYM!" she read out loud. "See?" she said to Darcy. "I bet that's why only two kids have signed up so far. It sounds so boring."

"You've got a point," Darcy agreed.

"I know I've got a point," Stephanie said. "Now, if they had a party while kids were repainting the gym, or . . ." Her words trailed off as an idea came to her.

"Or what?" Darcy said.

"What if the teachers made it a *sleep-over* painting party?" Stephanie asked. "Everyone would show up for that."

"A *sleep over*?" Darcy echoed. "I don't know if the teachers would go for that, Steph."

"But it'd be so much fun." Stephanie's mind was churning with ideas. "We could order pizza, play CDs, and paint all night long. Plus, it would spice up my article for *The Scribe*. There'd actually be something to report."

"You know, Steph, that does sound pretty cool," Darcy said. "You should talk to the teachers about it. And here's your first chance," she added. Mrs. Nugent, their phys ed teacher, was walking toward them.

The two friends ran up to the gym teacher just as she was about to blow her silver whistle.

"What is it, girls?" Mrs. Nugent asked in her usual no-nonsense tone. She ran her fingers through her short white hair.

Stephanie explained her idea.

Mrs. Nugent burst out laughing. "An overnight painting party for ninth-graders?" she repeated. "Stephanie Tanner, that's a hoot!"

Stephanie blinked. "I didn't mean it as a joke, Mrs. Nugent. I . . ."

Mrs. Nugent laughed harder. "Can you imagine what would happen if you put a bunch of ninth-graders inside a gym for a night with buckets of paint?"

Stephanie and Darcy exchanged looks.

"They'd paint," Stephanie mumbled.

"That's right! They'd paint everything *but* the walls," Mrs. Nugent said. "Good try, though, Stephanie," she added. Then, before Stephanie could get

4

in another word, Mrs. Nugent wiped the tears from her eyes and gave a loud blast on her whistle.

"Line up near the foul line, girls," she boomed. "We're going to practice jump shots today."

"Sorry about that, Steph," Darcy murmured. The two of them followed the rest of the class over to the foul line. "I thought it was a really good idea."

"Me, too," Stephanie said. "But obviously Mrs. Nugent doesn't. What does she think we'll do? Finger-paint the walls like a bunch of kindergartners?"

Darcy shrugged. "You know how teachers are sometimes, Steph. They don't trust kids to act mature."

"You know what?" Stephanie said as another idea came to her. "I'm supposed to interview the principal, Mr. Thomas, for my article this afternoon. I'll tell him about my idea. I bet *he'll* like it."

Just then a tall girl passed the basketball to Stephanie. She caught it and quickly dribbled it up to the foul line and took a shot.

Swoosh! The ball dropped cleanly into the net.

"Nice shot, Stephanie," Mrs. Nugent called.

"Thanks," Stephanie replied. It was a good sign, she decided. The next point she'd score would be when Mr. Thomas gave her the go-ahead for the sleep-over painting party.

*   *   *

"Go right in, Stephanie." The secretary held open the door to the principal's office. "Mr. Thomas will see you now."

Stephanie stepped into the principal's office. Mr. Thomas was leaning back in his chair and smiling cheerfully. Yup, she thought. Luck is definitely with me.

"Hello, Stephanie," he said. "How's *The Scribe*'s star reporter?"

"Fine," Stephanie said. She sat down in one of the big leather chairs that faced the principal's desk. "Thanks so much for letting me interview you for my story."

"My pleasure," Mr. Thomas replied. "We certainly want the Big Cleanup Week to be successful."

"That's exactly how I feel, sir," Stephanie began. "That's why I wanted to tell you my idea for encouraging more student participation."

"Excellent." Mr. Thomas beamed. "I want to hear all about it."

"Well . . ." Stephanie said. "As you know, one of the activities involves getting students to repaint the gym."

Mr. Thomas nodded. "That's right. It's about time the gym got a face-lift."

"I was thinking that maybe, if you made it a sleep-over painting party—"

"Oh, was that your idea?" Mr. Thomas chuckled. "Mrs. Nugent told me about it in the faculty lounge today." Mr. Thomas smiled. "A sleep-over! All the teachers thought that was a really good joke, Stephanie. In fact, we had a good laugh when we heard it."

A good laugh? Stephanie felt her cheeks turn bright pink. The teachers had all been laughing at her?

"Don't get me wrong," Mr. Thomas went on. "I'm delighted you're thinking of ways to get more students involved. I just don't think a sleep over is the right way to do it."

"But, Mr. Thomas . . ." Stephanie began. She tried to keep her voice calm, but she could feel herself getting angry. "So far only two kids have signed up to paint the gym. A sleep-over painting party would encourage a lot more kids to show up."

"Maybe a lot of kids would show up—but how many would actually paint the walls?" the principal asked. "Plus, we'd need to have chaperons to supervise. Not to mention the fact that . . ."

Mr. Thomas went on for several minutes about why they couldn't possibly have a sleep-over painting party at school. Stephanie found herself tuning him out. He was making it sound as though the students were three-year-olds instead of fourteen. As if they couldn't do anything without messing up.

"Enough about that," Mr. Thomas finally said. "You came to interview me for the article you're writing. That's what will really help to increase student participation."

"Okay," Stephanie mumbled. She reached into her backpack for her notebook. Like a good reporter, she asked her questions and jotted down Mr. Thomas's replies. But her mind kept going back to how he and Mrs. Nugent had both thought her idea was a joke. Why couldn't they trust a bunch of ninth-graders to behave at a sleep-over party?

I thought this was John Muir Middle School, not preschool! Stephanie fumed. *I'm sick of being treated like a little kid. And I'm going to do something about it!*

CHAPTER
2

◆ ◀ ▶ ◆

Stephanie was still fuming when she got home from school that day. She walked into the living room. Alex and Nicky, her four-year-old cousins, were spread out on the living room floor, coloring on large brown sheets of paper.

"Stephanie!" they called when they saw her.

"Hi, guys," Stephanie said. She stopped to admire their drawings. Then she went into the kitchen, where her uncle Jesse was unloading the dishwasher. Jesse was her mother's brother. He had come to live with Stephanie, her sisters, and their dad after their mother had died. When he and Becky got married and had the twins, they moved into the apartment attached to the house.

"Hey, Steph," Jesse said. "What's wrong? You look *mucho* bummed out."

"I am," Stephanie said. She dropped onto a kitchen chair and told him about her meeting with the principal.

"Sounds pretty grim," Jesse remarked.

"It is," Stephanie grumbled. "I can't wait to get to high school or college." She followed Jesse as he brought a plate of cookies out to the twins. "At least there they won't treat me like a baby anymore."

"Who's a baby?" Michelle called. Stephanie's nine-year-old sister hurried down the stairs, her strawberry-blond ponytail bobbing.

"Not us!" cried Alex.

"We're big!" Nicky added.

"For four-year-olds," Michelle agreed, grabbing a cookie.

The door to the kitchen swung open. D.J., Stephanie's eighteen-year-old sister, walked into the living room and yawned. D.J. was wearing her plaid nightshirt. Her short ash-blond hair was tousled.

Stephanie sighed. She'd really wanted to just talk with Jesse about her problem. But it was kind of hard to get time alone with anyone in a house shared by nine people!

Things got even more crowded a second later.

The front door opened, and Stephanie's dad, Danny, and her aunt Becky came in together. Danny and Becky were co-hosts on a morning TV show called *Wake Up, San Francisco*. They were just coming home from a long day at the studio.

"Hey, everybody," Aunt Becky said as the twins threw themselves into her arms.

Stephanie said hello to her father and aunt, then turned back to her older sister.

"D.J., are you just getting up?" she asked. It occurred to her that D.J. was still in her pajamas.

D.J. shook her head sleepily. "I pulled an all-nighter to finish my English paper." She nodded toward a stack of papers sitting in a clear folder on the side table by the door. "I finished it at five this morning. It's for medieval literature, and it's worth a third of my grade. It absolutely had to be turned in today."

"Then why aren't you at school, handing it in?" Danny asked.

"I have afternoon classes today," D.J. mumbled. Suddenly, alarm filled her face. "What time is it?"

"Three-thirty," Aunt Becky replied, checking her watch.

"Three-thirty!" D.J. shrieked. "My class is at four! I'll never make it."

"Hurry and I'll drive you," Becky offered. "If we don't hit traffic, you'll get there by four."

D.J. charged up the stairs. In less than five minutes she ran back down in a shirt and jeans. She threw her hairbrush into her khaki backpack as she went. "Ready," she announced breathlessly.

As Becky and D.J. rushed out, Joey Gladstone walked in.

"Hi . . . bye," Joey said to Becky and D.J. with a bewildered grin. "Where were they going in such a hurry?"

Joey was one of Danny's best friends. They'd been roommates in college. Joey had moved into the house at the same time as Jesse. Like Jesse, he'd moved in to help Danny after the girls' mom died.

"D.J. has to turn in her college paper but she was running late," Michelle explained.

Stephanie smiled to herself. She might as well just give up on the idea of a private chat with her uncle. With so many people always coming and going, it sometimes felt as if she were living in the middle of a busy train station. None of her friends had houses that were so hectic—or so much fun.

Joey turned to the table by the door. He began looking through his mail. "D.J. has *so much* work this term," he said. He flipped through the envelopes and flyers. "She's got another paper right here." He looked down at it and read. "Medieval literature."

"Medieval literature?" Stephanie echoed, jumping to her feet.

"Yep," Joey confirmed.

Stephanie snatched up the paper and raced to the door.

"D.J., wait!" she shouted.

But she was too late. She got to the door just as the back of Aunt Becky's car turned the corner. "Oh, no!" Stephanie wailed. "This is the paper that D.J.'s supposed to turn in today!"

"Oh, well," Joey said. "She'll have to turn it in tomorrow."

"She can't," Stephanie told him. "It's due today and it's worth a third of her entire grade."

Poor D.J., Stephanie thought. This was awful. "I know!" she said. "We could bring it to her! Can someone give me a ride?"

"That's an idea . . ." Jesse agreed. He looked at Danny. "If you don't mind me leaving the twins with you, I wanted to take Joey to the station to show him some new ads." Jesse and Joey were co-hosts of a radio show called *The Rush Hour Renegades.* "We could drop you off at the college, Steph, and pick you up on our way back."

"Sounds good," Joey agreed. "Steph, do you know where to find D.J.?"

"She showed me the Student Center once," Stephanie replied. "I'm sure someone there can help me track her down. Let's go."

"Wait a minute, guys." Danny held up a hand to stop them. "I'm fine with watching the twins. But, Stephanie, are you sure you can find your way around the campus?"

"Absolutely, Dad," Stephanie said.

"I don't know," Danny said doubtfully. "It's a big campus, and D.J.'s class could be anywhere—"

"Dad, I'm not a baby!" Stephanie insisted.

"Maybe not," her father said with a smile. "But you'll always be my baby. I can still remember that time when you were a toddler, and you got lost going from the kitchen to the bedroom. You stood on the stairs and screamed . . ."

Stephanie rolled her eyes and raced out the front door behind Joey and Jesse. Even her own father was treating her like a three-year-old today!

A short while later, Jesse pulled the car up in front of a low brick building.

"Want me to come in with you?" Jesse offered.

Stephanie unbuckled her seat belt and began to

climb out of the backseat. "No way! I'll be fine," she said firmly.

Joey unbuckled his seat belt. "I'd better go with you."

"No!" Stephanie insisted. "I can handle this."

"Do you have money?" Jesse asked.

"Yes! But why would I need money?"

"In case of an emergency," Jesse frowned. "We'll pick you up right here in a half hour—after we're done at the station. But you know our phone number there if you need us, don't you?"

"Yes. I know it, but don't worry. I'm not going to call you," Stephanie said firmly.

Jesse reached into the glove compartment and took out a pad and pencil. He wrote down the number at the station. "Just in case," he said, handing it to her.

Joey reached into his jacket pocket and pulled out a handful of change. "Take this in case you have to call on a pay phone," he said. He pressed the coins into her hand.

"I *have* money, and I'm *not* going to have to call you!" Stephanie cried. "Come on, you guys! Trust me."

"Of course we trust you," Jesse insisted. "We just worry."

Stephanie climbed out of the car. "You don't have to worry! I can do this."

"All right," Jesse said. "See you in a half hour."

"Okay," Stephanie said.

"Bye, Steph." Joey still sounded reluctant to leave. "We'll see you later."

"See you," Stephanie said.

As they finally drove away, Stephanie sighed with relief. She was alone at last—and on a college campus!

CHAPTER
3

Stephanie's eyes widened as she stared at the campus. There were so many buildings! Most of them were old and made of brick. She wasn't sure which one was the Student Center.

The buildings surrounded a big, grassy rectangle, where a group of students were playing Frisbee. Another group sat studying beneath a tree. Stephanie watched as one boy pointed to something in his notebook, then leaned over and kissed the girl beside him. Studying for college classes looked like a lot more fun than studying for middle school.

Suddenly, Stephanie felt very, very young. For the first time in her life, being fourteen seemed terribly embarrassing. Quickly, she grasped the ends of her denim shirt and knotted them together in front, hoping that made her look older. She fished in her backpack for a tube of lipstick and some eye shadow.

"Here goes," she murmured after touching up her makeup.

She walked up to a girl who was hurrying along one of the paths between the buildings. "Excuse me," Stephanie said. "But do you know where I could find the Student Center?"

"Right behind you," the girl answered without slowing down.

Stephanie spun around. Sure enough, brass letters on the building behind her read MAXWELL STUDENT CENTER.

Stephanie pushed open the big double doors. The Student Center was even more hectic than her house.

Students rushed up and down the stairway in the lobby, chatting with one another and laughing. Rock music blared from a speaker.

To Stephanie's right, about twenty students sat on couches, watching three TVs, each tuned to a different channel. A young man walked through the center handing out leaflets and repeating, "Save our Science Center. Lecture and protest at six tonight." A young woman was putting up a poster for a free movie that weekend. And through glass doors behind the TV area, Stephanie could see a little coffee house called the Campus Cafe.

Wow! Stephanie thought. A smile spread slowly across her face. This was so cool! It was *completely* different from middle school. The students seemed different, too. Their clothes were more casual but also more sophisticated. They all seemed so together and sure of themselves. None of them, she told herself, even had to think about anything as dumb as the Big Cleanup Week.

For a moment Stephanie almost forgot all about finding D.J. Then she remembered the term paper in her hand.

I'd better find D.J.'s class right away, she thought.

A woman with thick black hair was doing paperwork at a wide desk. A sign in front of her read INFORMATION.

Stephanie hurried over to the desk. "I have to get this paper to D. J. Tanner," she said. "It's urgent."

"What class is she in now?" the young woman asked.

"I'm not sure. Could you look it up for me?" Steph asked.

"I'm sorry." The woman shook her head. "I don't have that information."

"D.J.'s a freshman and she has short blond hair," Stephanie blurted out. "She's pretty and—"

The woman held up her hand. "Whoa. That's not going to help me. There are thousands of students on this campus. There's no way I could know them all."

This woman didn't know D.J.? Stephanie blinked. But everyone knew D.J. when she was in high school. Boy, college sure was different.

"What should I do?" Stephanie asked. She held up the paper. "She's going to be in big trouble if she doesn't hand this in today."

The woman suddenly looked more sympathetic. "You could try the registrar's office," she suggested. "Maybe they have a copy of her schedule."

"What's a registrar?" Stephanie asked. "Is that where you register for classes?"

"Right," the young woman replied. "Just go to West Hall, on the other side of the quad."

The quad? Stephanie thought.

The woman must have seen the blank look on her face. "The quad is that big open quadrangle in the middle of campus," she explained. "The registrar's office is on the tenth floor of West Hall."

"Thanks," Stephanie said. She headed outside,

crossed the quad, and gazed at the row of tall buildings. "One of them has to be West Hall," she told herself.

She quickly found Zambrini Hall and Science Hall and the modern languages building. "Great," she muttered. "Where did they hide West?"

After almost ten more minutes of searching, Stephanie still hadn't located it.

"Excuse me," she called to a boy as he dashed past. "Where's West Hall?"

"Don't know," he replied, not even slowing down.

The next two people she asked couldn't help, either. Stephanie blew a strand of hair from her face. Didn't anyone know where the registrar's office was? How could students not even know the buildings at their own college? This was so crazy!

An older man passed, his arms full of books. "Do you know where West Hall is, sir?" she called to him.

He looked puzzled for a second, then said, "Oh, you mean the administration building. It's behind Zambrini. Go down the path and make a left."

"Thanks so much!" Stephanie called. She began jogging along the path to West Hall. A few minutes later she was taking the elevator.

The tenth floor was completely deserted. Where did everyone go? Stephanie wondered. She walked down the shadowy hallway, checking each door. At the end of the corridor she found an office with a sign that read REGISTRAR.

Stephanie stuck her head inside. "Hello?"

No one answered. There wasn't anyone inside.

Stephanie threw up her arms in frustration. "This is ridiculous!" she muttered.

"It sure is," said a voice from behind her.

Stephanie whirled around, and her breath caught in her throat. Behind her was one of the cutest guys she'd ever seen. He had broad shoulders, dark, wavy hair, and hazel eyes.

"Uh . . . uh," she stammered.

The boy frowned as he looked at the clock. "It's just twenty minutes past four, and they're already gone for the day," he said. "They're supposed to be here until at least four-thirty. It really messes people up when they close early."

"It's really messing me up," Stephanie said.

"Why?" the boy asked.

Stephanie held up her sister's term paper. "D.J. forgot her paper. If she doesn't hand it in by the end of class, her professor won't accept it. And now I won't be able to find her class, and she's going to fail, and she stayed up all night to write this. It's just awful!"

"Wow! You're a good friend," the boy commented. "By the way, my name's Eric."

"Hi, Eric. I'm Stephanie."

She was about to explain that she was talking about her sister, not her friend, when Eric held out his hand. "Let's see."

"See what?"

"The paper."

Stephanie handed it to him.

"Medieval literature, huh?" he said. "I have a friend in that class." He thought for a second, then his face brightened. "I know where it is. It's in Doherty Hall!"

Stephanie's spirits lifted. "Great!" she said.

Eric smiled. "It's got to be the same class. Professor Thourston's got a big medieval English lecture class over there right now. And my friend also had to turn in a paper today."

"Is it far from here?" Stephanie asked. She glanced at the clock.

"Kind of," Eric said. "But I'll take you," he offered.

"*You'll* take me?" Stephanie echoed.

"Sure," Eric said. "Come on."

Stephanie couldn't believe her luck. A college boy—a *cute* college boy—was leading her across campus! It almost made her glad that she had trouble finding her way by herself!

CHAPTER

4

◆ ◂ ◆ ◆

Stephanie stepped into the elevator with Eric. She suddenly felt very nervous. She didn't know what to say to a boy who was a college student. "This is so nice of you," she finally mumbled. Her face turned red. She sounded ridiculous!

But Eric didn't seem to notice. "No problem," he said cheerfully.

She followed him outside. Eric pointed to a cluster of buildings in the distance. "Doherty Hall's the tall one. The campus is really confusing when you're new," he went on.

"I'm not exactly new," Stephanie began to explain.

"What do you mean?" he asked.

"I go to middle school," she admitted. But her

words were drowned out by the rumble of a campus bus passing by. Eric cocked his head toward Stephanie, straining to hear.

"You went to school at Middleton?" he said. "That's out of state, right? I figured you were a transfer student, since it's spring semester and you're kind of lost."

Transfer student? Stephanie knew she'd heard D.J. use that phrase before. She was pretty sure it meant someone who started at one college then changed to a different one. "No . . . I—"

"I transferred my first year, too," Eric said. "I found I didn't like being so far from home, so I came back here. Now I can go to college and still see my old friends from high school. I like it better that way. But not everyone's the same. How about you?"

"I live at home, too," Stephanie said. "But I don't really have a choice because—"

"Money problems, I hear you," Eric filled in.

He thinks I'm a college freshman! Stephanie realized. *He really believes that I transferred from some college called Middleton.*

"I have to work after school to earn extra money," Eric was saying. "It's not easy with my schoolwork and being the editor of the campus paper and all."

"You're on the school paper?" Stephanie said. "I write stories for my paper, too."

"You wrote for the Middleton paper? Cool!" Eric said. "That's actually why I was in West Hall. I'm writing a piece about how administrative services on campus can be improved. I heard a rumor that the registrar's office had been closing early, so I went up to verify it."

Stephanie couldn't help grinning at him. "A good reporter always checks the facts," she said.

"Definitely," Eric agreed. He smiled back at her with so much warmth that Stephanie felt her heart race.

He sure is gorgeous, Stephanie thought. *And nice, too!*

"Listen, Stephanie," Eric said. He turned onto one of the narrow footpaths. "Since you have journalism experience, why don't you come work on our paper?"

Stephanie hurried to keep up with his quick pace. "I couldn't," she started to say. "I—"

"Why, because you're new?" Eric waved his hand dismissively. "Everyone's new at first," he told her. "I know! You could write an article on the freshman experience. It would help the Orientation Committee get ready for their program next year."

"The what?" Stephanie blurted out.

Eric gave her a quizzical look. "You know, the Orientation Committee—the people who help freshmen the first week of school. Remember?"

It was flattering being mistaken for a freshman— *very* flattering. But Stephanie knew she couldn't let Eric continue to think that.

"Look, Eric," she said. "The reason I didn't know about the Orientation Committee is because I wasn't there to—"

Eric lightly hit his forehead. "Of course! I forgot. You're a transfer student, so you missed orientation week completely."

"That's not exactly why," Stephanie tried again. "I'm not usually on campus. I just came today to deliver this paper because—"

"Because you're a great friend," Eric finished for her. "Not everyone would do that. I admire loyalty, I really do. There aren't many people who would go all out for a friend."

"She's actually . . . uh . . . like, my sister," Stephanie said. She had to make him understand.

"It's great to feel that close to one of your friends," Eric said. "I mean, so close that she's *like a sister*."

Stephanie couldn't help it. She laughed. Once this guy got an idea in his head, it wasn't easy to shake it out.

"Hey, by the way, those are cool earrings," Eric said.

Stephanie touched the hoops in her ears. "Thanks," she said with a smile. *Is he flirting with me?* she wondered. First he'd invited her to write for the paper. Now he was admiring her loyalty *and* her earrings.

A few minutes later they reached a building with tall arched windows. "The lecture hall's on the second floor," Eric said. "When you get up there, just go in the first door on the left."

"Great. Thanks," Stephanie said. She hesitated. She couldn't believe that she was just going to say good-bye to him now. And after that she'd never see him again.

"So . . . what do you think of my idea?" Eric asked abruptly.

"What idea?"

"The story," Eric said. "The article on freshmen for the paper."

"I can't write that article, Eric," Stephanie said reluctantly. "Really. I . . . I . . . I just can't." But all she could think about was how exciting it would be to see Eric again. And to work together on the college paper.

"Sure you can," he said.

"No, I can't," Stephanie insisted. "I don't know anything about the freshman experience."

Eric rolled his eyes. "Transfer students are still freshmen, Stephanie. You can write about your own experience as a freshman transfer, and then interview other freshmen," he argued. "Besides, I like to have an even number of reporters from each year on my staff—and I could really use some more freshmen."

Stephanie sighed. "Listen, Eric, I'd love to do it, but—"

"I'm not going to listen," he said. He raised his hand as if to block all her objections. "The article is due on Tuesday. Promise you'll think about it some more, and I'll call you tonight."

Stephanie's throat went dry. This gorgeous, nice, totally cool college student wanted to call *her?* There was no way she could say no now. "O-okay," she replied.

Eric held out a notebook and pen, and she wrote down her phone number. She hoped he didn't notice the way her hand shook.

"Great," he said with a smile. He glanced down at his watch. "You'd better get in that lecture hall, or you'll miss your friend. Class is nearly over. Talk to you later."

With a wave, he headed back up the path and disappeared from sight.

Stephanie let out a deep sigh. *When he calls I'll tell him I'm in ninth grade,* she promised herself. But—until then—she could just daydream, couldn't she? She could see herself walking through the campus beside Eric. Everyone would see them together and know that they were the star reporters for the school paper. She could even imagine going into the newspaper office for her first real assignment. Eric would introduce her to the rest of the staff as "the best freshman writer this paper has ever seen." He'd assign her a front-page article. And then afterward—

Stephanie was startled out of her daydream by a gentle breeze. It blew through her hair and rustled the papers she held in her hand.

"Oh, no!" she cried.

She'd been so busy picturing herself in college, she'd forgotten all about what she was doing there. Nervously, she glanced at her watch. There were only ten minutes before D.J.'s class ended. She had to find her sister right away!

CHAPTER
5

◆ ◀ ▮ ◆

Stephanie pushed open one of the swinging doors that led to the lecture hall. It squeaked noisily, and she cringed. The last thing she needed was to announce her arrival to the whole class.

But to Stephanie's surprise and relief, only a few students in the back rows turned around. They glanced at her with mild curiosity, then looked away.

Stephanie stood behind the last row of seats in the huge lecture hall. She looked around, and her jaw slowly fell open in shock. In all her life she'd never, ever seen a class this huge. About five hundred students sat in the rows of seats. It looked more like a theater than a classroom. Down below, a thin man wearing a bow tie stood at a podium. He was talking about a famous writer named Chaucer. All around Stephanie, students frantically scribbled notes.

"Chaucer's *Canterbury Tales* embodies the epitome of the medieval literary goal," the professor lectured. He had a loud, stern voice. Stephanie could see why D.J. wouldn't want to make him angry. He glared at a student who had coughed, then went on. "The mix of high-minded content intertwined with the humorous and bawdy gives voice to a transitional yearning for both laughter and nobility emerging from the dark days of the plague."

What? Stephanie could barely follow what he was talking about. No wonder D.J.'s struggling with this class, she thought.

The professor droned on. Stephanie scanned the sea of students, searching for her sister. This *had* to be the right class. But where was D.J.?

Stephanie looked up and down the rows for an empty seat. She found one on the aisle and slid into it. She craned her neck, looking for her sister.

The girl beside Stephanie slumped in her seat and let out a long, miserable sigh. "Boring," she whispered in a low singsong voice. She twirled a long dark strand of her hair around a finger.

"I can barely understand a single word he's saying," Stephanie whispered.

The girl grinned. "I know what you mean," she agreed.

"Do you know D. J. Tanner?" Stephanie asked hopefully.

The girl looked at Stephanie. She had beautiful violet-colored eyes. "Sorry."

"Well, D.J.'s in this class and I have to get her paper to her," Stephanie explained.

The girl glanced at the title of the paper in Stephanie's hand. "Definitely," she agreed. "She has to turn that in if she wants to pass."

Desperately, Stephanie looked around the enormous room again.

"Maybe you can just hand it in for her," the girl suggested.

Stephanie turned to her. "Me?"

The girl shrugged. "Sure. Why not?"

Stephanie hesitated. "I don't know the teacher and it's not my paper—"

"Then give it to me," the girl said. "I have to hand mine in at the end of class, anyway."

"You really don't mind?" Stephanie asked, relieved. She had not wanted to approach that professor. "That would be so great."

"No problem," the girl said. "By the way, I'm Sara Bendix."

"I'm Stephanie," she introduced herself. "I'm not in this class."

"Lucky you." Sara sighed. "You must have registered on time. I registered late, and this was one of the only courses left. Now I know why. It's *awful!*"

Stephanie smiled in surprise. Someone else had mistaken her for a college student! But she didn't really want to lie—especially since Sara was being so nice. "Well, actually, I . . ." Stephanie began. Her words trailed off as the professor dismissed the class. Students started getting up from their seats and picking up their things.

"Wait for me," Sara told her. "I'll hand these papers in and be right back."

Stephanie wanted to say that she had to run. She'd been on campus for nearly an hour. She was sure that Uncle Jesse and Joey were waiting for her. But Sara was already gone. She was hurrying down toward the professor against the crowd of students who were headed for the doors.

It seemed rude not to wait. Stephanie stayed in her seat and looked around for D.J. But there was no sign of her sister in the throng of students.

Stephanie crossed her fingers. She hoped that

D.J. hadn't realized she'd forgotten her paper and gone back home for it.

Most of the students had left by the time Sara returned. "All set," she announced, gathering her books. "So, Stephanie, are you doing anything tomorrow night?"

"No. Why?" Stephanie asked.

"My dorm is having a party. Hindman Hall, third floor. Eight o'clock."

A dorm party, how cool! Stephanie thought. But there was no way she could go to Sara's party— not when she had to write that article on the Big Cleanup Week for *The Scribe* over the weekend. Besides, her father would never, ever let her go to a college party. "Thanks, I can't," Stephanie said quickly.

"Why not?" Sara asked. She headed for the door. "There'll be tons of kids there."

"I'm sure there will be, but I—"

"Eric!" Sara called out suddenly.

Stephanie's heart thudded as she looked up. Sure enough, Eric was headed toward them. "Hey, Sara!" He turned. "Stephanie! We keep bumping into each other today. Do you and Sara know each other?"

"We just met," Stephanie replied. "What are you doing here, Eric?"

"I have class in this lecture hall next period," he told her. "I figured I'd get here a few minutes early."

"Eric," Sara began. "Tell Stephanie she has to come to our party. She says she can't make it for some mysterious reason."

Eric gazed at her with his hazel eyes. In this light, they almost looked green. "You have to come to the party, Stephanie," he said.

"Will you be there?" Stephanie asked him.

"Of course. I'm in the same dorm as Sara," he explained. "And it'll be a lot more fun if you're there."

Oh, man, Stephanie thought. He *does* like me. This was total proof! "Well, uh, maybe I can make it," she murmured.

"Good." Eric flashed her a big smile. "We can talk about the article you're going to write for me at the party," he said. Then he turned to Sara. "I'm trying to get Stephanie to write for the *Express*."

"Cool," Sara said. "You should do it, Stephanie. It's a really good paper. They won two college journalism awards last year."

Stephanie couldn't believe it. Both Eric and Sara were so great. They treated her like she was smart and grown-up. As if she could do anything that she wanted.

"I'm not sure about the article, but I'll definitely

try to get to the party. Hindman Hall, eight o'clock," she repeated.

"Be there or be square," Eric teased. "Oh, and bring your friend, D.J., if you like. I'd better get to class," he added, checking his watch. He backed away down the hall. "I won't call you tonight, Stephanie, because I'm going to see you tomorrow. Right?"

"Right," Stephanie called back.

"And I'm going to get your article on Tuesday, right?" Eric continued.

Sara gave Eric a small shove. "Leave Stephanie alone, and maybe she'll think about it," she turned to Stephanie. "I'm so glad you're coming to the party. Now I have to run to class. See you tomorrow!"

"Bye!" Stephanie said, waving as Sara took off. "Thanks for the invitation."

For a long while Stephanie stood there in the hall. A big grin lit her face. She had not only managed to hand in D.J.'s paper, she had made two new friends. And the best part was they treated her as if she were a mature, intelligent college freshman—instead of a three-year-old.

I love college. It's sooo much better than middle school, Stephanie decided. *And I can't wait until . . .*

"Stephanie! What are *you* doing here?"

CHAPTER
6

♦ ◀ ◆ ♦

Stephanie whirled around. D.J. was hurrying toward her, a shocked expression on her face. "What are you doing here, Steph?" D.J. repeated.

"I came to deliver your term paper. I just handed it in to your medieval literature professor."

D.J.'s jaw dropped and her face lit with relief. At first she didn't say anything. Then she grabbed Stephanie in a bear hug. "Oh, I can't believe it! I can't believe it," D.J. cried. "You're the greatest sister on earth! The best!"

"Uh . . . D.J.," Stephanie said in a muffled voice. "You're squeezing me so hard, I'm suffocating."

D.J. quickly let go. "Sorry, Steph," she said, laughing. "You don't know what I've been through. I didn't realize the paper was missing until I got to the lecture hall. Then I figured I must have dropped it. So I've been all over campus searching for it. Once I decided it was hopeless, I tried to run to class to explain to Professor Thourston. I'm so glad I don't have to, though. He's not exactly the type to understand about missing papers."

"You're not kidding," Stephanie agreed. "That is one scary-looking teacher."

"I still can't believe it," D.J. went on. "How did you ever find my class and get up the nerve to deliver the paper?"

"I had some help," Stephanie replied.

"From whom?" her sister asked.

"Just by accident I met the greatest guy," Stephanie explained. She went on to tell D.J. about Eric. When she got to the part about writing an article for the school paper, D.J.'s smile faded.

"You told him you couldn't do it, right?" D.J. demanded.

"Well, I . . ." Stephanie fumbled. "I tried to tell him, but he didn't get it," she said.

"Why not?" D.J. asked.

"I guess you could say he has this habit of jumping in when people are talking," Stephanie said weakly. She didn't bother to tell D.J. that a part of her hadn't wanted to tell Eric the truth.

"Stephanie," D.J. said warningly. "You'd *better* make him understand."

Stephanie felt a flicker of annoyance. After everything she'd just done for D.J., why did D.J. have to act like the big sister, bossing her around?

"I *could* write the article if I wanted to," Stephanie said stubbornly.

"You're in middle school!" D.J. reminded her. "How could you possibly write about the freshman experience? That's ridiculous!"

"It's not ridiculous!" Stephanie shot back. "I've heard you talk about what it's like to be a freshman. I know a lot about it. And I'm a good writer. You've said so yourself!"

"But you're only in middle school!" D.J. said again.

Stephanie tossed her hair. "Obviously I'm mature enough to convince two college students that I'm a freshman," she informed her sister.

"Who else thought you were a freshman besides this guy Eric?" D.J. demanded.

"A girl," Stephanie stated. "A girl I met in your class. You don't know her, and she doesn't know you."

Stephanie had intended to tell D.J. about the

dorm party that she'd been invited to. She was even going to invite D.J., as Eric had suggested. Wouldn't that be cool—Stephanie taking D.J. to a dorm party as *her* guest! But now that D.J. was being so crabby, Stephanie changed her mind. The way things were going, D.J. would just freak out and tell her that she couldn't go.

"Listen, D.J., I can't talk about this anymore," Stephanie said. "Jesse and Joey are waiting for me. They're probably really worried about where I am by now. I've got to go and meet them."

"Fine," D.J. said with scowl. "We'll talk about this some more when I get home."

"If we have to," Stephanie said coolly.

D.J.'s expression suddenly softened. "Steph, thanks again," she said. "I really appreciate it. Okay?"

"Whatever," Stephanie said, pushing open the door to Doherty Hall. She knew D.J. was trying to apologize. But Stephanie wasn't quite ready to forgive her.

Outside, Stephanie hurried back to the Student Center. Jesse was parked at the side of the building. He waved frantically when he saw Stephanie approaching. "Where have you been?" he demanded.

"I'm sorry I'm late," Stephanie replied. "It took me a while to track down D.J."

"Joey's inside, searching for you," Jesse said.

Stephanie was about to go inside the Student Center to look for Joey, when he hurried out. His worried expression relaxed as he spotted her.

"There you are!" he exclaimed. "Did you get the paper to D.J.?"

"Mission accomplished," Stephanie told him.

"Wow, Steph." Joey sounded impressed. "You found your way around campus on your own?"

"No problem," Stephanie said proudly. She climbed into the backseat and looked around as Jesse drove off. She'd had so much fun today—she couldn't wait to come back tomorrow night!

That night, after dinner, Stephanie went up to her room early. D.J. was still at school—probably studying—and Stephanie didn't want to be around when she got home. She wanted to be left alone—to dream about Eric and to think about seeing him again tomorrow night at the party. She felt as if a whole new world were opening up to her. She walked into the room she shared with Michelle, her head in the clouds.

"So how was college?" Michelle asked.

"Amazing," Stephanie replied in a dreamy voice.

"What's so amazing about it?" Michelle asked.

"Everything," Stephanie answered.

"I guess you really liked it," Michelle said, impressed.

"I *loved* it," Stephanie corrected her. "I wish I went there instead of middle school. You know, I've been thinking about it, and I've decided that I'm ready for college."

Michelle gave her a doubtful look. "I don't know, Steph. D.J. says college is really hard. Don't you think you need to finish the other grades first?"

"Well . . ." Stephanie considered Michelle's question. "I didn't understand much of what D.J.'s professor said today," she admitted. "But neither did the girl next to me. And she really *is* a college student. So, that proves I could do the work."

Michelle's brow wrinkled as she tried to follow Stephanie's logic. "I guess so," she said.

"You know something, Michelle?" Stephanie stretched out on her bed. "No wonder I've been so unhappy in middle school lately. I really belong in college, where people respect other people's ideas and treat students like adults. Maybe I can talk to my guidance counselor about it on Monday."

Michelle shook her head as she climbed into bed with a book. "I have to tell you something, Stephanie."

"What?"

"I think you've gone crazy."

"Michelle!" Stephanie cried.

"What you're saying makes no sense," Michelle insisted. "How can a person go from ninth grade right to college?"

Stephanie knew that Michelle had a point. "Well, maybe I could skip a year of high school or something," she said.

"You get good grades, but it's not like you're a genius, Steph," Michelle pointed out. "They skip only really, really smart kids. You're going to have to wait to go to college."

"Oh, what do you know," Stephanie muttered grumpily. She turned away from Michelle and rolled over onto her side.

My sisters just don't get it, Stephanie decided. Since D.J. and Michelle lived with her, they still thought of her as a kid. So did her dad, and so did Jesse and Joey and even Aunt Becky. None of them noticed how mature she'd become.

Darcy and Allie will understand, Stephanie told

herself. Plus, they'll go crazy when they hear how I got invited to a college party.

She jumped out of bed and scurried down the hall to D.J.'s room. D.J. had her own phone line. Stephanie wasn't supposed to use it, but she needed some privacy for this call.

She phoned Darcy first and told her everything that had happened.

"That's too cool, Steph!" Darcy exclaimed. "I wish *I* could go to college party."

"You can. Come with me tomorrow night," Stephanie suggested.

"But I wasn't invited," Darcy protested.

"*I'm* inviting you," Stephanie told her. "It's going to be a huge party. No one will know the difference."

"Does that mean I'll have to pretend I'm a college student, too?"

"Of course," Stephanie replied. "But you won't believe how easy it is, Darcy. I wasn't even trying, and I fooled everyone!"

"You didn't try at all?" Darcy asked.

"Well, maybe a little," Stephanie admitted. "I mean, I put on a little makeup, and I tied up my denim shirt. But it wasn't a big deal. Come over tomorrow," she went on. "It's Saturday, so there's no school. I'll help you get ready."

As soon as Stephanie said those words, she remembered something: She was supposed to be working on her article for *The Scribe* tomorrow. *I'll work on it in the morning,* she decided, *and finish it on Sunday.* She'd definitely have it ready for Tuesday, which was when she was supposed to turn it in.

"I'm going over to Allie's house tomorrow morning," Darcy said. "Maybe you can come over and help both of us get ready. I bet Allie will want to come, too."

"Maybe," Stephanie said. Suddenly, she felt a little worried about involving Allie. Of the three friends, Allie definitely looked the youngest. She was very petite. Denim overalls were her favorite outfit. She didn't wear a bit of makeup, and she often wore her long reddish-brown hair in pigtails. Worse, she had a habit of giggling like a little girl. Some days she didn't even seem fourteen.

"I don't know if Allie could fool anyone," Stephanie murmured. "She looks awfully . . . young."

"I thought you said it was easy," Darcy reminded her.

"I did. It was," Stephanie admitted. "I'll see you guys tomorrow, okay?"

Stephanie hung up, still trying to figure out what

to do about Allie. Darcy would be fine, but Allie was such a . . . such a kid.

Stephanie headed back to her room, troubled. Eric would take one look at Allie and realize she didn't belong at the party. It wouldn't take long for him to figure out that Stephanie didn't belong there either.

Stephanie sighed. What choice did she have? If she told Allie not to come, she'd hurt her feelings. There was no way Stephanie would do that. Besides, she reasoned, tomorrow I'm going to tell Eric that I'm fourteen, anyway.

But later, as Stephanie drifted off to sleep, all she could think about were Eric's soft hazel eyes and his perfect smile.

Maybe she could find a way to let him think she was eighteen for just a little while longer. . . .

CHAPTER
7

◆ ◀ ◆ ◆

The next morning Stephanie woke early, especially for a Saturday. She had a mission to accomplish. She jumped out of bed, dressed quickly, gulped down some breakfast, then hurried over to Allie's house.

Stephanie rang Allie's doorbell and waited impatiently for someone to answer it. She was about to ring it a second time, when Allie came to the door. Her hair was mussed, and she was wearing a long white nightgown.

"Stephanie," Allie said in a half-yawn. She rubbed her eyes sleepily. "What are you doing here?"

"Hi, Allie." Stephanie stepped into the front hall and looked around. "Is Darcy here yet?"

"It's only eight o'clock, Steph," Allie pointed out. "My parents are still asleep. What's going on?"

"I figured we should get an early start if we're going to fix you up."

Allie's green eyes widened. "What do you mean, fix me up?" she said. "Fix me up for what?"

Stephanie grinned. "A college party! Wait till you hear about what happened while I was at D.J.'s school."

Stephanie followed Allie into the kitchen. Allie poured a bowl of cereal while Stephanie began her story.

"Awesome," Allie declared when Stephanie told her about Eric and Sara inviting her to the party. "It's so cool that your father said you could go."

Stephanie inhaled sharply. She hadn't stopped to think about how her father would react to her going to a college party. But now that she did think about it, she was pretty certain he wouldn't like the idea. "He . . . uh . . . hasn't exactly said I could go," she admitted.

"He hasn't?" Allie looked up from her cereal.

"He doesn't really know about it," Stephanie mumbled.

Allie raised one eyebrow. "Is he *ever* going to know about it?" she asked.

"Possibly not," Stephanie admitted.

Allie gave Stephanie a long look. It was a look that Stephanie had seen many times before, and she didn't want to see it now. Allie was very sensible. And this look meant that she was about to say something very sensible.

"You shouldn't go, Stephanie," she blurted out. "You're going to get in big trouble."

"Look, Allie," Stephanie tried to explain. "You didn't see Eric. If you had, you'd know why I *have* to go to this party. He's really cute and smart and really nice, too. And being on campus is so great. There are movies and plays and a cafe—and no one treats you like a three-year-old—"

"It's still not worth it," Allie broke in. "If your father ever finds out that you sneaked out to a college party, he'll go ballistic. You'll be dead meat."

Stephanie frowned. This was exactly why she'd been nervous about telling Allie about the party in the first place. It wasn't just Allie's appearance, Stephanie realized now. It's Allie's attitude. She's afraid to try new things, Stephanie thought. Maybe Allie just wasn't ready for anything more sophisticated than middle school.

"Did you forget that today is Litter-Free School

Day?" Allie asked. "We're supposed to be at the school at nine-thirty."

"Oh, no!" Stephanie said. She *had* forgotten about it. Completely. But there was no way she could fit it into her schedule now.

"I can't go," she told Allie. "I'm totally focused on getting ready for this party."

"You have to go." Allie spoke through the mouthful of cereal. "We signed up for the poster-making committee. Remember?"

Stephanie's spirits sank. Now that Allie mentioned it, she did remember signing up for the committee. But she wished she hadn't remembered. All she wanted to think about right now was the party. And at some point during the weekend, she had to squeeze in writing her article for *The Scribe.*

"That's why Darcy is coming over," Allie went on. "We were going to walk over to the school together. She said she'd help me carry some poster supplies I bought. We thought you were going to meet us there."

"Why didn't Darcy mention it when I spoke to her last night?" Stephanie asked. "We talked about getting ready for the party at your house."

Allie shrugged. "She must have thought you were talking about later in the day. I mean, I doubt

Darcy expected you to be here at eight in the morning, Steph."

Stephanie just stared blankly at her friend. How had her plans for a sophisticated college weekend suddenly become so complicated?

"Darcy will be here around nine," Allie said, looking at the kitchen clock. "We can head over to school then."

Stephanie made a face and circled one finger in the air. "Oh, goody," she said sarcastically. "Then we can all skip off to school and draw posters. I can hardly wait," she grumbled. It was hard to imagine anything more childish.

Stephanie dabbed at her poster with a paintbrush soaked in red poster paint. She, Darcy, and Allie had joined five other kids in the cafeteria. All of them were painting posters to be hung around the school. At the moment she was painting the petals of a tulip she'd drawn in the middle of the poster board. Above the flower she'd printed the words: KEEP JOHN MUIR CLEAN. DON'T LITTER!

"Why don't you put a ladybug on the tulip?" Darcy suggested. "That would be cute."

"Oh, adorable," Stephanie replied without enthusiasm.

"It was just an idea," Darcy said, sounding miffed.

"Sorry," Stephanie apologized. "This is just so . . . juvenile."

"Oh, come on, Steph. It's fun," Allie said as she drew whiskers on a kitten.

Stephanie rolled her eyes. "If you say so."

Mr. Merlin, Stephanie's media skills teacher, wandered over to their table. He was one of the teachers who was helping out at Litter-Free School Day. "Don't look so excited, Stephanie," he kidded her. "Your enthusiasm is overwhelming."

"She's not really into this today," Allie said.

"Oh, really?" Mr. Merlin laughed. "I couldn't tell."

"Face it, Mr. Merlin," Stephanie said in a bored tone. "This isn't exactly challenging work. A kindergartner could paint posters."

"Actually, I don't think kindergartners could spell all these words," Allie pointed out, smiling a little.

"All right!" Stephanie snapped. "A second-grader could do it. Is that better?"

Allie nodded.

"Actually, I have something more challenging for you, Stephanie," Mr. Merlin said.

Stephanie's eyes lit up. "You do? What?"

"I've gotten permission to paint a couple of murals on the walls," Mr. Merlin said. "Would you girls like to start one on the blank wall to the left of the girls' locker room?"

"That sounds like more fun than posters," Stephanie agreed. "I know! We could paint a total seventies retro scene, with a disco ball and people in bell-bottoms, and—"

"Whoa," Mr. Merlin cut her short. "It has to be a mural depicting a girls' soccer game—in a beautiful, litter-free soccer field."

"You're kidding!" Stephanie groaned. "But that sounds so . . . dull."

"Mr. Thomas agreed to the murals on the condition that he decided the subject matter," Mr. Merlin explained. "I think he was worried about what students might come up with on their own."

"It figures," Stephanie muttered. "He treats us as if we're babies."

"Mr. Thomas is being a little cautious," Mr. Merlin said evenly. "And you have to admit, it is probably a good idea to decide what's going to be in the mural ahead of time."

"Come on, Steph. It'll be fun," Darcy coaxed her. "Let's go work on the mural."

"I suppose it's better than doing this." Stephanie gave in.

The girls followed Mr. Merlin to the wall where they were to begin the mural. "Start sketching," he told them. He headed down the hall. "I'll be back soon with paints."

After a brief planning discussion, the girls began sketching their scene with light pencil strokes. But after just a few minutes, Stephanie stopped drawing. The only thing that interested her was getting back to the college campus.

"What's the matter?" Darcy asked, glancing at Stephanie.

"I can't pay attention to this, not with the party coming up tonight," Stephanie said. "We should be home planning what we're going to wear." She looked at Allie, who was wearing her overalls again. "Do you own anything that looks sort of . . . well, more grown-up?"

"I don't think so," Allie admitted. "But it doesn't really matter."

"It does matter, Allie," Stephanie argued. "You can't go to a college party looking like a middle-school kid. Then everyone will suspect I'm a middle-school kid, too. And then—"

"Relax, Steph," Allie cut in. "I'm not going to the party."

"You're not going?" Stephanie echoed. "Why not?"

"My parents would ground me forever me if I got caught sneaking into a college party," Allie explained. "I don't want to get into trouble."

Stephanie nodded. One part of her was disappointed, but another part—a bigger part—was relieved. Now she didn't have to worry about Allie looking too young.

She gave Allie a sympathetic glance. "That's okay. I understand. Darcy, what about you?"

Stephanie hoped that Darcy would say yes. Darcy was so tall and beautiful. It wouldn't take much to make people think she was a college student.

"It makes me a little nervous," Darcy admitted, "but I want to go. It sounds really fun."

"Great!" Stephanie said. "Then let's sneak out of here right now and go get ready."

"Steph!" Darcy protested. "The party isn't until eight."

"It's going to take time to put on our makeup and figure out what to wear," Stephanie insisted.

Darcy shook her head. "Mr. Merlin's coming back with the paint. We can't just ditch this."

Stephanie took one more look at the soccer ball and player that she'd sketched and made up her mind. "I'm leaving before Mr. Merlin comes back," she told her friends. "I'll get myself ready, and then I'll be able to help you get ready later, Darcy. Okay?"

Darcy shrugged. "I guess."

"Come to my house by six-thirty," Stephanie told her. "This is going to be so great. Finally, I'll be hanging out with people my own mental age."

Allie whispered something.

Stephanie looked at her. "What did you say, Allie?"

Allie kept her back to Stephanie as she continued drawing. "I just wondered what you meant by *your mental age*."

"I've been thinking about it a lot," Stephanie explained patiently. "And for some reason, I've matured at a faster rate than other kids our age. I'm not sure why it happened," she went on, "but going to the college yesterday totally opened my eyes. College is where I belong."

"Come on, Stephanie," Darcy scoffed. "You don't really believe that, do you? I thought this party was just a big goof."

"No way, Darcy," Stephanie said. "This is serious. I'm sick of being treated like an immature middle-school kid with crazy ideas. I want to meet some people who are going to have more respect for my thoughts."

"You've totally flipped, Steph," Allie commented dryly.

Stephanie felt herself losing patience. "I haven't *flipped*, Allie," she explained. "I'm simply going through something that you're not ready to understand yet."

"Oh, excuse me," Allie said. "I guess my *mental age* isn't as advanced as yours."

Stephanie didn't know what to say. She'd thought Allie would understand. Instead, it seemed as if Allie disapproved of her. But she didn't have time to argue just then. "See you guys later," she said.

"Okay," Darcy replied. "I'll be over at six-thirty."

"Later," Allie chimed in.

Stephanie checked the hall to make sure Mr. Merlin wasn't coming, then she took off for the exit doors.

She walked home, trying to imagine what the party was going to be like. But she couldn't stop thinking about Allie. She was acting as if Stephanie was doing something wrong.

Well, I'm not, Stephanie told herself. *And I'm not even going to think about it.*

College students are too independent and mature to let their friends' opinions influence them. And from now on, I'm going to act like a college student!

CHAPTER
8

◆ ◄ ◆ ◆

"I hope this works," Darcy said in a worried voice. She stood in front of Stephanie's mirror and studied her reflection. "Are you sure my hair looks okay?"

Stephanie had swept Darcy's black hair back from her face, added some gel, then held it in place with a thin black leather headband. She'd crimped the hair behind the headband, using an electric crimper.

"You look amazing," Stephanie assured her. "Just like that model in the magazine. She wore her hair exactly like this."

"I know, but she's a model," Darcy pointed out.

"You could be a model if you wanted," Stephanie

said. She meant it, too. Darcy didn't seem to realize how pretty she was. Stephanie studied her friend's face. It had taken her forty minutes to make it up, using the makeup bag she'd borrowed from D.J.'s dresser.

"I know what you need," Stephanie said. She rummaged through D.J.'s bag yet again. Seconds later, she held up a tiny pot of sparkly coppery eye shadow. She dabbed a finger in the pot, then rubbed a coppery smudge under each of Darcy's delicate eyebrows. "There! Perfect!" she announced.

Darcy studied her face in the mirror. "It *does* look kind of cool." She giggled. "I like it!"

Stephanie stood beside her friend. She stared critically at herself one last time in the mirror. "We definitely look like college students," she decided.

Stephanie had used the crimping iron to crimp the top layers of her own hair. The rest she let hang loosely around her shoulders. She'd lined her eyes with a violet pencil. Finally, she'd used a deep-red lip pencil to line her lips and then she'd filled them in with a brown-toned lipstick.

Both girls had decided to wear jeans and over-sized shirts—but had added some jewelry. "Do these earrings make too much noise when I move?" Darcy asked. As she shook her head, the teeny-tiny bells that made up her earrings softly jingled.

Stephanie leaned in to listen. "No. They're fine."

Stephanie glanced at her watch. It was 7:45. The day had passed so quickly. She'd never found a moment to work on her article for *The Scribe*. *I'll work on it tomorrow,* she told herself. Then she turned to Darcy. "We'd better go."

"I hope my parents don't call your house," Darcy said worriedly. "I told them I'd be here all night."

"Don't worry," Stephanie said. "My dad and Aunt Becky are out at a business dinner. Michelle is staying at a friend's house, and D.J.'s in some lab at school, working on a chemistry experiment."

"What about Joey and your uncle Jesse?" Darcy asked.

"They're upstairs with the twins in Uncle Jesse's apartment," Stephanie replied. "They're going over some stuff for their radio show. I told them that you and I would be hanging out in my room tonight. There's no way they'll check on us."

"Are you sure?" Darcy still looked nervous.

"Positive," Stephanie said. "We got really lucky tonight, Darcy. No one's going to suspect a thing." With that Stephanie pushed open her bedroom door and cautiously checked the hall. All clear.

Then she and Darcy hurried down the hall, down the stairs, and out the front door. They didn't say a word to each other or slow down until they reached the city bus stop two blocks away.

"This bus will drop us off right on campus," Stephanie explained. "D.J. takes it to school all the time."

Thirty minutes later they climbed off the bus. "I saw a sign for Hindman Hall one block that way," Stephanie said, pointing to the left. "That's the name of Eric's dorm."

The path to the dormitory was well lit. In front of Hindman Hall, a small group of students stood talking.

"This should be a cool party," one of them was saying.

Stephanie nudged Darcy. "They must be going to the same party," she whispered. "Let's go in with them."

Darcy nodded, and they crowded into the elevator with the group. Stephanie could feel her heart hammering with excitement. She was really doing it. She was fitting in with the college scene.

Seconds later, the elevator opened onto a hallway that was jammed with people. Loud music blared from speakers somewhere down the hall.

Steph and Darcy followed the music into a big,

open room. Sodas and baskets filled with pretzels and popcorn were set up on tables. A silver strobe light flashed, making everyone look as if they were caught in a slow motion. In the middle of the room, Steph could see a large group of people dancing.

"Wow!" Darcy murmured as she stared around in amazement.

"This is so cool," Stephanie breathed.

A boy with blue hair and a nose ring passed them. He nodded his head as if he were listening to music only he could hear. A girl with very pale skin dressed all in black swept dramatically past them.

Stephanie couldn't believe how interesting and mature everyone looked. She could already tell that this was going to be a lot more fun than a middle-school party.

"Let's get some soda," Stephanie said. She poured a cola for Darcy. And that's when she spotted him. Eric was standing in the hallway, talking to Sara. "There he is!" she whispered.

Darcy looked up. "That's him?" she said, staring at Eric, openmouthed. "Whoa, Steph. He *is* really cute."

Eric had spotted Stephanie, too. He smiled and waved for her to come over.

"I'll be right back," Stephanie told Darcy. Her heart was racing with excitement. She felt as if all her dreams were coming true.

"Don't leave me," Darcy pleaded, panic in her voice. "I don't know what to do or who to talk to." She gripped Stephanie's arm tightly.

"I'll be back in five minutes, I promise," Stephanie said. She didn't want to abandon Darcy, but she wasn't ready to introduce her to Sara and Eric— not until Darcy had relaxed a little.

"Hi, Steph." Eric greeted her with a friendly smile. "Glad you could come."

"Me, too," Sara said. "Have you eaten yet? There's a sushi platter in room one twelve, and room one sixteen has some veggie platters with great dips." Then Sara rattled off five more rooms with different kinds of food in each. Stephanie had never even heard of half the things Sara mentioned.

"It all sounds delicious," Stephanie said. She thought she sounded totally lame, but she didn't know what else to say.

"So, how's that article coming?" Eric asked.

"Um . . ." Stephanie froze. *Come on, Steph,* said a voice inside. *Tell him the truth. You're only in ninth grade.* But somehow Stephanie's mouth refused to say the words.

"I . . . uh . . . didn't really say I'd write the article, Eric," she said, trying to stall.

"That's true. But I know you will," he replied. "A *real* journalist can't resist the chance to write an interesting article. And I know a real journalist when I meet one."

Was he calling her a *real* journalist? Once again Stephanie imagined herself on staff, working in the newspaper office to beat a deadline. Eric, she imagined, was standing next to her, telling her how awesome she was. "Well . . . we'll see," she wavered.

"Come on," he said, taking her arm. "I'll introduce you to some freshmen that you can interview for your article. We'll be right back, Sara."

"See you later," Sara said.

With his hand still on her arm, Eric led Stephanie into a dorm room where a group of kids sat perched on the bunk beds. Stephanie's heart raced. The touch of Eric's hand on her arm was such a thrill. And he'd seemed so happy to see her. . . . *He really likes me*, she thought happily.

"Hey, everyone," Eric said. "This is Stephanie, and she's going to write an article about the freshman experience."

A few of the kids groaned. Others rolled their eyes.

"Exactly," Eric said. "So could you help us out and tell her what it feels like to be a freshman here?"

Eric handed Stephanie a notepad, and she found herself taking notes. Most of the students gave answers like, "nervous," "confused," or "lost."

Stephanie could definitely relate—that was exactly how she'd felt when she first arrived on campus. *Hey,* she thought suddenly. *Maybe I can write this article.*

Stephanie lost track of how long she spent talking to the freshmen. But when she and Eric walked back into the hall, she suddenly had a sinking feeling. *Uh-oh,* she thought. *I left Darcy alone for much longer than five minutes!* She hoped Darcy wasn't too mad at her. Frantically, she gazed around, trying to find her friend in the crowd.

"Oh, no!" she gasped suddenly.

"What is it?" Eric asked.

Stephanie didn't reply. Instead, she just stared at Darcy in horror.

Darcy stood in the middle of a circle of girls. Of all the things she could possible be doing, she was twirling a silver baton! Stephanie groaned. Darcy looked like a five-year-old showing off for a group of camp counselors.

"Steph?" Eric prodded her. "What's up?"

"It . . . it's nothing," Stephanie said. "I'll be right back." She darted over to Darcy, who had just tossed the baton into the air. Quickly, Stephanie snatched it away before Darcy could catch it.

"Hey!" Darcy cried indignantly. "Why did you do that?"

Stephanie grabbed Darcy's arm and pulled her away from the crowd. "I have to talk to you," she said tensely through clenched teeth.

"What is your problem?" Darcy shot back.

"Nobody in college twirls batons, Darcy," Stephanie hissed. "That's a dead giveaway that you're only in middle school! Where on earth did you find that thing?"

"A girl—a *college* girl—lent it to me," Darcy informed her. "For your information, Stephanie, she was telling me that she performs at halftime during football games. *College* football games," Darcy went on. "And I was showing her a routine that I know. So, just chill out, okay?"

"I've never seen baton twirling at a college football game," Stephanie replied sullenly.

Darcy gave her a haughty look. "Well, maybe you don't know as much about college life as you think you do."

"Look, Darcy, I'm sorry," Stephanie said. "I overreacted, okay?" Then she rummaged in her jeans pocket and pulled out a tube of lipstick. "Put this on. Yours has worn off."

Using a window as a mirror, Darcy quickly reapplied her lipstick. Stephanie told her all about Eric and her freshmen interviews.

"Cool," Darcy said. She seemed to have gotten over being angry. "Go back and hang out with him. I don't mind, Steph. Really."

"Are you sure?" Stephanie asked.

"Yep. Go ahead," Darcy insisted. "I'll be fine."

"Thanks a lot, Darcy," Stephanie said gratefully. She squeezed her friend's hand, then hurried away to find Eric. Eric was at the other end of the hall, talking to some guys he knew.

"Hi," Stephanie said shyly.

The other guys all gave her friendly smiles. "Eric's been telling us about you," said a boy with a red buzz cut.

"I hear you're going to work on the paper," said the one named Dave.

Stephanie felt herself blushing. "I'm just writing this one article," she replied quickly. "But, after that, I won't be able to—"

Eric draped an arm over her shoulder. "The article will be great. Stephanie's going to be a regular contributor to the paper—mark my words."

Stephanie barely heard what Eric was saying.

The only thing she was aware of was that Eric had his arm around her, and was praising her in front of his friends.

This was so much more than she'd even hoped for. It was as though for years now she'd wanted to step through this one magical door that would change her life. If she could only find her way through that door, her life would be sophisticated and glamorous and romantic and exciting. And now Eric had just given her the key.

I've got to find Darcy so that she can see this, Stephanie thought. *And so later she can tell me that I wasn't dreaming!*

Stephanie glanced around the crowded hallway. Darcy has to be here somewhere, she thought. Maybe she's talking with someone or dancing.

Stephanie's eyes widened as she finally caught sight of her friend. It was even worse than before. Darcy was playing pat-a-cake with another girl!

Pat-a-cake? Stephanie blinked in disbelief. This time Darcy wasn't even acting like a ninth-grader—she was acting like a toddler!

"Excuse me," Stephanie murmured, slipping out from under Eric's arm. She had to stop Darcy before Eric noticed what Darcy was doing!

CHAPTER
9

◆ ◂ ◆ ◆

"I'm leaving!" Darcy fumed an hour later. She stomped to the elevator bank and punched the down button.

"I don't see why you're so mad," Stephanie said, following her.

"You don't?" Darcy exploded. "First you grabbed that baton from me. Then you told me not to play hand games with someone who happened to be very interested in learning more clapping games. Did I mention that she's about to start working in a day care center as part of her child psychology course?"

"Only about fifty times," Stephanie muttered. "How was I supposed to know, Darcy?"

Darcy ignored the question. "Then you yelled at me for teaching a girl to make gum-wrapper chains," she went on. "And last but not least, you embarrassed me by telling me not to giggle—even when that guy was telling jokes."

"You could have just smiled. You didn't have to giggle so loudly," Stephanie insisted.

"Excuse me," Darcy snapped. "But can I please have fun my own way?"

Stephanie sighed. She wished she could make Darcy understand how important this party was to her.

"It was just that you were acting so . . . middle school," Stephanie tried to explain. "I didn't want you to give away our age."

"You're the one who's giving yourself away by acting like a lunatic!" Darcy shot back. "Eric must think you're crazy—the way you kept rushing back and forth between him and me!"

"I told him I had a friend with a problem," Stephanie admitted.

"I do have a problem—you!" Darcy said. The elevator doors parted and she stepped inside. "But now I don't have it anymore. Bye!"

Stephanie sighed as she watched the elevator doors close again. She felt terrible that she'd upset Darcy and that Darcy was going back home alone.

But it isn't my fault, she told herself. *Darcy was acting like a kid, and I didn't want Eric to notice.*

Just then Eric walked over to her. "What's wrong, Stephanie?"

"Oh, my friend with the problem got upset and left," she explained. "I feel terrible."

"She'll be okay," Eric said. "Sometimes people need to deal with things by themselves."

"I guess," Stephanie said. She gazed up at Eric and felt her bad mood fade. Maybe now that she didn't have to worry about Darcy for the rest of the party, she could actually enjoy herself a little more.

"Want a soda or something?" he asked.

"Sure," Stephanie replied. They began walking together toward the table with soft drinks. But as they turned a corner in the hallway, Stephanie froze. Was she imagining it? No, definitely not. She'd just spotted D.J. at the end of the hall!

"What's the matter now?" Eric asked.

"I—I—I—I," Stephanie stuttered. "I . . . feel sick all of a sudden," she blurted out. "I'll be right back."

Stephanie darted away from Eric, desperate to find a place to hide. Her mind raced. What was D.J. doing here? She was supposed to be in some sort of science lab. Had D.J. already spotted her?

Stephanie ducked into one of the bedrooms. "Excuse me," she said to the three girls standing near the closet, talking. "I have to get my jacket." She hurried past them into the closet, and then quickly slid the door shut from the inside.

Stephanie could feel her heart pumping hard. Sweat trickled down her back. It was hot and cramped in the dark, narrow space. The closet was jammed full of clothing. An angora sweater tickled the end of her nose. She felt a wooden hanger digging into the side of her neck. This was awful! she thought. How long was she going to have to stay in there?

Stephanie forced herself to stay put. She knew that she couldn't let D.J. see her. D.J. would be furious that Stephanie hadn't told Eric and Sara the truth. And knowing D.J., she'd probably tell their dad, too!

After what seemed like forever, the closet door began to move. Stephanie shrank backward, flattening herself against the back wall. But it was no use. Suddenly, she heard a familiar voice. "You're right, thanks," D.J. said to someone. "She is in the closet."

The door opened wide. The other girls had left the room. It was just the two of them.

"Hi," Stephanie said in a quavering voice. "What are you doing here?"

"Me?" D.J. glared at her. "What are *you* doing here?"

"I asked you first," Stephanie said with a nervous laugh. "You're supposed to be working on a school project."

"We finished up at the biology lab and then walked over here," D.J. explained. She placed her hands on her hips. "Your turn."

"*I* was invited," Stephanie said. "By Eric and Sara."

"The ones who thought you were a freshman?" D.J. demanded.

"Yes," Stephanie said. She felt a little more confident. She really hadn't done anything terrible. She'd been invited to a party and she'd come. That was all there was to it.

For a few minutes D.J. didn't say anything. She just stared at Stephanie as if she were trying to decide what to do.

"Do you have a bag or anything?" D.J. finally asked.

"No. Why?"

"Because we're going home. Right now," D.J. replied in a matter-of-fact tone.

"No way, D.J.! I'm not leaving!"

D.J. gripped Stephanie's arm. "Yes, you are," she said firmly.

Stephanie yanked her arm away. "You can't make me."

"Watch me," D.J. said in a cold voice. "You're not supposed to be here."

"Why not?" Stephanie demanded.

"Because you're *not* a college student. You're in ninth grade—remember?"

"Shhhhh," Stephanie hissed, glancing around frantically. "Someone will hear you."

"I don't care if they hear me. You're coming home with me, and that's that!"

Stephanie folded her arms. She was sick of D.J. acting so bossy. It was time D.J. learned that she couldn't just order her around.

"No," Stephanie said stubbornly. "I'm not moving. And there's nothing you can do about it."

"Oh, yes, there is," D.J. said. "I'll find this Eric guy and tell him why you have to leave. Then I'll go home and have Dad or Joey or Jesse come back and get you. Either you can make me do that, or you can just come with me right now. Your choice."

Stephanie glared at her sister. D.J. wasn't giving her a choice at all. She couldn't believe D.J. was treating her this way. She was never going to speak to her again. Not ever!

"Come on." D.J. took hold of Stephanie's wrist

and pulled her along, out of the room and down the hall, which was still noisy and crowded with partying students. Thankfully, Eric wasn't around as they made their way to the elevator bank.

An elevator came quickly and they took it down to the lobby, where D.J. called a cab to come get them.

Stephanie slumped in her seat as they rode home. Her arms were folded tightly across her chest. Next to her, D.J. stared out at the night through the cab's windows. For a long time, neither of them said a word. But as the cab turned down their block, Stephanie felt her stomach clench. "Are you going to tell Dad?" she asked.

"I might," D.J. replied flatly. She was still looking out the window. "I haven't decided."

"Please don't, D.J.," Stephanie begged. "You know he'll freak."

D.J. didn't look at Stephanie, but she seemed to be considering her words. "Dad does overreact sometimes," she admitted. "Still, I don't know . . ."

"Please," Stephanie asked desperately. The cab was getting closer to their house. "D.J., come on, please, please, please."

"I said, I don't know," D.J. repeated impatiently.

Reluctantly, Stephanie kept quiet. She knew that

anything else she might say would only make D.J. angrier.

A moment later the cab pulled up in front of the house.

Stephanie held her breath. If D.J. told on her, she would be in major trouble. She'd probably be grounded for life. And she'd never see Eric again.

CHAPTER
10

◆ ◂ ◆ ◆

D.J. didn't say a word until she reached for the doorknob. Then she turned around. "I won't tell this time, Stephanie, but . . ." She gave her sister a warning look. "If I ever see you on campus again, I will tell Dad."

"Thank you so much, D.J." Stephanie said. She let out the breath she'd been holding.

"Do you know what a stupid and dangerous thing you did?" D.J. went on. "No one even knew where you were. What if something had happened?"

"Nothing would have happened," Stephanie said.

"You don't know that," D.J. shot back.

"Okay, okay," Stephanie said. "You're right." She was too relieved to argue with D.J.

D.J. studied her sister for a moment. "Oh, and one more thing. As payback for making me leave the party, I expect you to do my chores for a week."

"No problem!" Stephanie said. She knew she'd gotten off easy.

"Just don't do it again," D.J. reminded her as she opened the door. "I'm not kidding, Stephanie."

Inside, the house was unusually quiet. Stephanie hurried upstairs and shut the door to her room. She was glad that Michelle was sleeping over at a friend's house.

Stephanie flopped onto her bed and closed her eyes. Whew! What a night, she thought. She couldn't decide if more good things or more bad things had happened.

The good things were that Eric had definitely been happy to see her, she'd passed for a freshman, and now she wasn't in trouble. The bad things were that Darcy was mad at her, she was stuck with a week's worth of D.J.'s chores, and she still hadn't written her article on the Big Cleanup Week.

Suddenly, Stephanie sat bolt upright. Thinking about the article for *The Scribe* reminded her that she'd better get started on the article for the college paper, too. Eric was counting on her getting it done in time for the next issue.

Stephanie hurried over to the computer on her desk. There was another good thing about going to the party tonight, she realized. It had given her a short but very realistic college experience. Plus, Eric had helped her interview those freshmen.

The computer screen blinked on, and Stephanie clicked the mouse to create a file titled College Article. She pulled out the page of notes she'd taken and glanced at them quickly.

Life in college is very busy, she typed. *It's confusing, too. Being a freshman is hard. Very, very hard. Difficult, you could say.*

With a disgusted sigh, she hit the delete key and made all her words disappear. She started again.

Life as a freshman is different from what I expected. It's hard to describe really. Practically indescribable.

"Yuck," she said aloud, hitting the delete key once more. This wasn't going to be easy. Maybe she should try a more personal approach.

My life as a freshman would have been a total disaster if I hadn't met Eric. It's amazing that someone so handsome can also be so nice. Nice isn't really the word—wonderful beyond belief is more like it. He helped me when I was lost, befriended me when I was alone, and made my freshman experience absolutely fantastic.

"You can't write that," she mumbled. With a sigh, she once again deleted what she'd typed. Then she shut down the computer. Obviously, she needed a little more information before she wrote her article.

On Sunday morning Stephanie awakened to a loud knock on her door.

"Phone for you, Steph," her dad called.

Stephanie yawned as she climbed out of bed and picked up the phone. "Hello?"

"Hey, Steph." It was Sue Kramer, the editor of *The Scribe*. "I was just going over the layout for the next edition," Sue went on. "And I was wondering how long your article on the Big Cleanup Week is running."

"Well, I . . . I haven't really started it," Stephanie admitted.

"You haven't started it?" Sue echoed. "Stephanie, I need it by Tuesday at the very latest!"

"I know. And you'll definitely have it," Stephanie promised. "I'll be writing it today. I have tons of notes."

"I really hope so," Sue said. "Let me know how long it is as soon as you have a first draft."

"Fine, bye," Stephanie said. She shook her head as she hung up the phone. Why was Sue making such a big deal about the Big Cleanup Week? Didn't she know Stephanie had more important topics to write about?

The phone rang again and Stephanie snapped it up.

"Hi, it's Allie. How was the party?"

Stephanie was a little surprised, but glad that Allie had called.

She told her all about Eric and interviewing freshmen for her article. "Darcy and I had a fight, though," she added. "And I was busted by D.J. and dragged home. But it was still worth it."

"It was?" Allie seemed skeptical. "Oh . . . well . . . good . . . I guess. Listen, can you rehearse tomorrow after school?"

"Rehearse?" Stephanie's mind was a blank.

"You know," Allie explained, "for the skit that we wrote for the Big Cleanup Week."

"Oh, right," Stephanie said.

"We have to perform it this Friday at the assembly for the close of the Big Cleanup Week," Allie reminded her. "So we'll meet at my house after school tomorrow. Okay?"

"Okay." Stephanie sighed. She tried to sound more enthusiastic than she felt. "See you tomorrow."

She hung up the phone. When she and her

friends had written the skit together the week before, they'd all thought it was hysterically funny.
Now the whole thing just seemed dumb. Stephanie
winced as she imagined Eric and Sara in the audience. If they ever knew she was in something so
silly and immature . . .

Nope, she decided, there was simply no way.
She couldn't do the skit. She'd just have to think
of a way to make Allie and Darcy understand.

On Monday, Stephanie could barely concentrate
on her classes. All her brain power was focused on
the article she had to write for the college paper.
Somehow she had to get it done and it had to be
excellent. She had to prove to Eric that she was a
"real" reporter.

I'll go back to campus after school today, she decided. *That way I can do some more research.*

In the hallway after her first class, Stephanie
spotted Darcy walking ahead of her. For a moment
she felt angry with her, the way she'd felt Saturday
night. But Stephanie couldn't stay angry with
Darcy. Darcy was too good a friend.

She quickly caught up to her. "Are you still mad
at me?" she asked softly.

Darcy stopped and scowled at Stephanie. Then

her expression softened. "I guess not. But you were a major pain, let me tell you."

"I know. I'm sorry," Stephanie apologized.

"Maybe I overreacted a little, too," Darcy said. "I should have remembered that it was a big night for you."

Stephanie nodded. "I know I was acting a little crazy," she admitted. "It's just . . . I really like Eric and Sara. I guess I wanted to impress them."

Darcy gave her a sympathetic look. "Did you ever tell them how old you really are?"

"No." Stephanie shook her head. "Wait till you hear what happened."

The two friends walked down the hall, and Stephanie filled Darcy in on how D.J. had arrived at the party.

"You're kidding! You hid in the closet?"

Stephanie grinned. This time when she told it, the story actually seemed kind of funny. By the time she dropped Darcy off at her classroom, both of them were laughing.

"I'll see you at our rehearsal later," Darcy said as she walked into her math class.

The skit! Stephanie thought, her heart sinking. But she just nodded. They'd talk later. Right now, she was just glad that they were friends again.

*   *   *

The final bell of the school day rang, and Stephanie headed straight for her locker. She grabbed her books, then raced out of the school. She didn't stop running until she got to the bus stop. And she didn't really relax until she was on the bus that stopped at the college.

Twenty minutes later Stephanie was back in the Student Center, trying to track down some freshmen to interview. She approached two girls sitting near the TVs and told them she was writing an article for the paper. Then she took out a pen and her notebook. "What's the most difficult thing about being a freshman?" she asked.

"Registering for a required is stress city," one of them told her. "You want a cinch prof because you'll ace it, and that's good for your cume. But everybody wants the same thing. You know?"

Stephanie didn't know. She didn't have a clue as to what the girl was talking about. Quickly, she scribbled in her notebook: *Need cinch prof for ace cume*, and hoped she'd be able to translate the girl's comments later.

"Frosh are always dissed," another girl told her. "I can't wait to be a soph and get into electives."

Sophs wear electives, Stephanie wrote down. She guessed it was the brand name of jeans or something.

For the next hour, Stephanie continued her interviews. By the time she was finished, she had pages of quotes that she barely understood. All the unfamiliar terms and phrases made her head spin! Still, she refused to panic. All she had to do now was to go home and make sense of her notes.

Stephanie stuffed her notebook in her shoulder bag and went outside. She couldn't quite remember which way the bus stop was.

As Stephanie tried to orient herself, she noticed two girls on the other side of the quad walking toward her. She squinted hard. Something about them was familiar. They came a few feet closer and she could see them more clearly.

It was Allie and Darcy!

Stephanie suddenly remembered something— she was supposed to be at Allie's house, rehearsing for the skit! Somehow it had completely slipped her mind.

Then, coming out of the modern languages building, Stephanie saw another familiar figure approaching. Eric!

This time Stephanie panicked. She couldn't let Eric see her talking with her friends—especially Allie. She looked as if she was about twelve. And without makeup Darcy looked almost as young.

Stephanie spun around and headed back inside

the Student Center. Along the far wall she saw a bank of leather couches, where a few students sat reading. She ducked behind a couch, her heart beating fast. She waited, listening for the sounds of her friends' voices. All she heard was someone complaining about library hours.

Slowly, Stephanie rose to peek over the top of the couch. Darcy and Allie were standing on the other side of the room. Had they seen her come in? Stephanie wondered. Or were they just looking around, hoping to find her?

Stephanie felt her face turn bright red. She felt so guilty. She'd honestly forgotten all about the rehearsal.

Allie and Darcy stood in the doorway, looking helpless and confused. Stephanie couldn't help but remember how overwhelmed she'd felt the first time she entered the Student Center.

Maybe I should go and apologize, she thought. Eric was nowhere in sight, but still . . . Stephanie knew he was nearby. She just couldn't risk being seen with them.

Stephanie ducked her head back down and hoped her friends would leave soon. She promised herself that she'd call them the minute she got home.

When she glanced up again, she saw Allie and Darcy walking out the front door.

Whew! Stephanie stood up and took a breath. Thank goodness they'd left.

She was about to step out from behind the couch—when something made her freeze. Allie was walking back into the Student Center.

CHAPTER
11

♦ ◀ ◆ ♦

The next morning Stephanie woke up with a painful knot in her stomach. She'd hardly slept. All she'd done was toss and turn—and replay in her mind that awful moment when Allie had returned to the Student Center.

Stephanie had felt like a criminal who'd just been caught red-handed. Allie had glanced around the center one last time. She seemed to stare right at Stephanie. Then she'd simply turned and left again.

Stephanie had no idea if Allie had seen her or not. But she knew she'd let her friends down.

Joey walked by Stephanie's open door. "Rise and shine," he called cheerfully. "Michelle's already downstairs eating breakfast."

Stephanie took a deep breath. "Joey," she called.

He stepped into the room. "What's up?"

"I don't feel well enough to go to school today," she said in a weak voice.

Joey sat down on the end of her bed. "Did you eat anything unusual yesterday?" he asked.

Stephanie shook her head. "I don't think so."

Joey felt her forehead. "You don't have a fever," he noted. "Is something bothering you, Steph?"

"Yes. My stomach," she groaned.

"I mean something emotional," he said. "When I was younger, I used to get stomachaches whenever something made me anxious. The first few times I stood up on a stage and told jokes, I had killer stomachaches beforehand."

"Well . . ." Stephanie hesitated for a second before blurting out the truth. "I think Allie and Darcy are mad at me."

"Why?"

Stephanie hesitated again. She couldn't exactly tell Joey everything.

"I forgot about a dumb skit rehearsal we had yesterday," she said.

He nodded. "Well, maybe you should go to school so that you can clear things up with them," he said. "Then it will be over with. I bet it makes

your stomachache go away. After my comedy rou-
tines were over, I'd feel just fine."

That was probably a good idea, Stephanie
thought, but, whatever the cause, her stomach really did hurt. "I just can't," she groaned, clutching
her stomach.

"All right," Joey said, getting up. "Stay home,
then."

Stephanie went back to sleep. When she awoke
an hour later, the house was quiet and her stomach
felt much better. But she felt even guiltier than she
had before. I really should be at school today, she
thought. She knew Joey was right—she should
have gone and faced her friends.

With a sigh, Stephanie got out of bed. *At least I
can use the time to get my articles done,* she decided.
She sat down at the computer to write her article
on the Big Cleanup Week.

*They want us to clean up our school, but they won't
let us do anything really fun like have a sleep-over
painting party,* she typed. *The teachers and administration think we're too young for that. Instead, we get to
make dumb posters and paint soccer murals. Like babies!*

I can't hand this in, Stephanie realized a minute
later. *Mr. Thomas would freak out.*

Stephanie deleted the file and started again. This
time she wrote about all the plans for the Big

Cleanup Week that she could think of—the posters, the murals, the cleanup day, and the upcoming assembly. She added a few quotes from her interview with Mr. Thomas. The article was barely one page long. Sue Kramer was expecting more, but there really wasn't much more to say.

Stephanie reread what she'd just written. Even she had to admit that it was dull and short on information. There was no way that this article would get more students to participate in the events.

But that's what I was trying to tell Mr. Thomas, she argued with herself. *He's the one who'd refused to listen to my idea for a sleep-over party. He's the one who refused to make things interesting.*

Stephanie printed out a final copy, then switched over to her file for the college article.

Many freshman students want a cinch prof to ace their cume, she typed, still not understanding what it meant. *Forget acing my cume—all I wanted was to find the right lecture hall.*

She sat back in her chair and grinned. "That's very cute," she congratulated herself. She knew from her work on *The Scribe* that finding a catchy opening sentence was sometimes the hardest part of writing a good article.

Many students use the words "lost," "confused," and

"nervous," to describe the freshman experience. That sure was me.

"Okay," Stephanie murmured with satisfaction. She could feel the wheels turning inside her head now. What she'd written was funny and personal. She could write this article, no problem.

Stephanie wasn't sure what to write next, so she closed the file. At least she had a strong beginning. Then she climbed back into bed and read a mystery novel until late in the afternoon.

By three o'clock Stephanie couldn't stop thinking about Darcy and Allie. She knew they'd be packing up their books and heading home.

I really do owe them an apology, she thought. *And I might as well get it over with.*

Stephanie got dressed and went downstairs.

"How's the stomachache?" Joey asked. He was sitting on the couch, reading a newspaper.

"I think you were right. I'll feel better after I talk to Darcy and Allie. That's where I'm going, to Allie's house."

Joey raised his eyebrows, about to say something, but Stephanie cut him off. "I know I should have gone to school today. It won't happen again."

"Good," Joey replied.

"Can I still go to Allie's?"

Joey hesitated. "Uh—I guess." He paused. Then

he smiled. "But as far as I'm concerned, young lady, you're going there to find out about your homework assignments, right?"

"Thanks, Joey. You're the greatest." Stephanie smiled back.

Stephanie pressed Allie's doorbell and waited. She felt more nervous than ever. Still, she knew she had to do this.

Allie answered the door, but she didn't say hi. She looked at Stephanie as if she were a stranger. Then she turned her back and walked into the house.

Well, at least she didn't slam the door on me, Stephanie thought. She followed Allie into the kitchen. Darcy was sitting at the table. The two of them had been snacking on a bowl of popcorn.

"Hi," Stephanie said. "What's up?"

"What happened to you yesterday?" Darcy asked. "You totally blew off our rehearsal."

"I know you were out of school today, but yesterday you seemed fine," Allie put in. "Where did you go?"

For a moment, Stephanie considered telling them she'd gone home sick. But these were her closest friends. She couldn't lie to them. "To be honest, I just forgot about the rehearsal," she admitted.

"You forgot? Or you wanted to go over to the campus?" Darcy asked.

Stephanie swallowed hard. They *had* seen her.

There was a long silence.

"We went looking for you at the college," Allie said softly. "Darcy thought she saw you there, but I wasn't sure."

"You hid from us, didn't you?" Darcy said.

"Um . . . well . . ." Stephanie stalled. She was trying to think of the best thing to say. "I . . . I didn't know what else to do. I suddenly remembered I'd forgotten the skit, and I panicked, I guess."

Allie shrugged. "Okay. I understand why you'd be embarrassed to see us after you forgot about the skit," she said. "Especially after the argument you had with Darcy the other night."

"Well, *I* don't understand," Darcy said angrily. "We're supposed to be your best friends. But now that Eric's come along, you want us to disappear."

"No, I don't," Stephanie protested.

"Well, that's how it feels, Stephanie," Darcy said coldly.

Stephanie felt herself getting angry. Why did

Darcy have to make such a big deal about this? She'd tried to apologize. "Look, Darcy," she said. "We don't have to do *everything* together all the time. It's so . . . immature!"

Darcy jumped up from her seat. "Would you stop calling me immature!" she shouted. "You're the one who's immature. You're the one who forgets about your friends. All so you can chase after some college guy!"

"I am *not* chasing him," Stephanie defended herself. "He wants me to write for his paper. And he likes me."

"Yeah, sure he does," Darcy scoffed. "He doesn't even know how old you really are."

Stephanie just stood there, glaring fiercely at Darcy. "That shows how much you know," she murmured. Then she turned to Allie. "I'll see you later, Allie. I'm going over to the college to talk to Eric for a few minutes."

"Do you want us to come with you?" Allie asked.

"No thanks," Stephanie said quickly.

"She doesn't want to be seen with us," Darcy explained.

Allie looked from Stephanie to Darcy, then back to Stephanie. "Is that true, Steph?" she asked.

"No," Stephanie lied. Her face burned. "I . . . I . . . just want to be alone."

"She's lying," Darcy said. "She didn't want to be seen with me at the party. She didn't want to be seen with us yesterday. And now she doesn't want to be seen with us again. Why don't you just admit it, Stephanie?"

"All right!" Stephanie exploded. "You're right, Darcy, okay? So I want Eric to like me. And I want to work on the college paper. What's the big deal?"

Allie blinked. "So you mean," she said slowly, "if you and Eric got to be a couple, you'd never want to hang out with Darcy and me again?"

"No, that's not—" Stephanie started to say.

"Yes, it is," Darcy jumped in. "That's exactly what it means."

"Oh, I can't talk to you two. You don't understand!" Stephanie whirled away from them. She ran out of the kitchen and out the front door.

She kept running until she reached the bus stop. *Allie and Darcy love being in middle school*, she told herself. But she just didn't feel that way anymore. Her life had changed the moment she'd stepped on campus. Now she knew how exciting college was. And she knew that middle school would never be that way. Stephanie just wished that her friends understood.

A city bus pulled up at the corner. Stephanie climbed aboard and paid the fare. She was going back to campus to find Eric, the only person who really appreciated the mature, grown-up person she was becoming.

CHAPTER
12

◆ ◀ ◂ ◆

Stephanie's pulse raced as she hurried down the hall in search of the office for *The Campus Express.* She had to see Eric again.

The newspaper office was located on the second floor of the Student Center. The hallway was nothing like the huge common room downstairs. It was quiet, nearly deserted. The only sound Stephanie heard was the faint buzzing from an overhead fluorescent light.

Stephanie reached the doorway marked THE CAMPUS EXPRESS. A stack of the most recent issues sat outside the door.

"Eric?" Stephanie called softly. She turned the doorknob, but it didn't open. The office was locked. Stephanie frowned. She thought Eric would be there all afternoon, editing.

Stephanie knelt down and peered through the mail slot in the door. Only one desk light was on. It was enough for her to see the inside of the room. "Wow," she murmured, impressed. It looked like the professional newspaper offices she'd seen on TV. There had to be at least ten desks, and every one had a computer on it. Rows of tall metal filing cabinets lined the far wall. On the right a long counter held a copy machine, a fax machine, and two printers. On the left a big drafting table displayed a layout for the next issue.

It couldn't have been more different from the *Scribe* office. If you could even call the closet-sized space with its one desk and one computer an office.

Stephanie suddenly realized how important Eric's job was. He was the editor in charge of this professional-looking newsroom.

He's amazing, Stephanie thought.

She reached down and picked up a paper. The headline read: *Administrative Services Flunk Out.*

That was the story Eric had been working on, Stephanie recalled excitedly. *Yes!* There was his by-line. *By Eric Maplewood.*

What a great last name, Stephanie thought. "Stephanie Tanner-Maplewood," she whispered, testing the sound of it. It definitely worked.

Her brow furrowed in concentration as she read Eric's article. It was really good. He had sure done his research. He knew the hours of every office on campus—and reported on which ones had been closed when they were supposed to be open for students. The article was loaded with numbers and statistics about how much money the state government contributed to keep the different departments running, and how much came from the students' tuition. Eric even showed how these amounts compared to similar departments in other schools. He seemed to know everything about the subject.

Stephanie stopped reading as a disturbing thought occurred to her: Was this the sort of article Eric expected from her? Did he want all these facts and numbers? Was she supposed to use words like "cumbersome," "bureaucratic," and "megalomania"?

She was getting that sick feeling in her stomach again. She didn't even know what those words meant!

"So what do you think of the article?" a voice asked.

Stephanie looked up into a pair of light hazel eyes. It was Eric!

"It . . . it's . . . it's awesome," she replied. "Absolutely awesome. You're like . . . a real reporter."

Eric laughed. She could see he was pleased. "I'd better be 'like a real reporter.' That's what I hope to be someday."

"Cool!" Stephanie said. "I'm sure you'll be great at it."

"Come on," Eric said. "Let's grab a soda."

"Okay," Stephanie said. She tried not to sound too excited. But inside, her pulse was racing. He'd actually asked her to have a soda with him!

Together they headed toward the soda machine. Stephanie couldn't help noticing all the other students who waved to Eric or said hi. He sure is popular, she thought.

She wondered what the other students thought when they saw her walking beside him. Everyone on campus was probably wondering if she was Eric's new girlfriend.

A smile slid slowly across her face. Dozens of girls were probably interested in Eric. But she— Stephanie Tanner—was the one he liked. She was the one he was standing right next to now.

"Here you go," he said, handing her a soda can. She reached into her pocket for change to repay him, but he waved her away. "My treat," he said with a smile.

My treat.

The words echoed in Stephanie's ears. That had to mean something. It was proof that he liked her.

Together, they popped up their flip tops and sipped their sodas.

"Hey, Maplewood!" a boy with long blond hair called out.

Eric waved, but didn't go over to talk to him. Instead, he stayed right where he was. His eyes were focused on Stephanie.

Stephanie was beginning to think she was in heaven. She was so happy, she even forgot all about how upset she'd been an hour before, when Darcy had been so angry at her.

"Uh, Stephanie," Eric said. "I need your article really soon. Do you think I could get it by tomorrow afternoon?"

The soda seemed to stick in her throat. Tomorrow? She started coughing hard.

"Steph?" Eric eyed her with concern. "Are you okay?"

"Yeah . . . yes . . ." she managed to answer. "Sorry. I swallowed my soda the wrong way." A moment later, she was able to breathe again. "Okay. That's better."

"So can you make that deadline for the story?" Eric asked.

She forced a smile. "No problem," she said, trying to sound confident. But inside, her stomach was churning. How in the world was she going to finish the story by tomorrow, when she had barely started it?

CHAPTER
13

◆ ◢ ◣ ◆

"Is something the matter, Stephanie?" her dad asked that evening at the dinner table.

"Is your stomach bothering you again?" Joey asked.

Stephanie looked up, startled. She suddenly realized she'd been staring at her uneaten mashed potatoes, lost in thought. "Me? . . . Uh . . . no . . . I'm fine. Why?"

"You looked like you were trying to burn a hole in your potatoes with your X-ray vision," Jesse joked.

Stephanie shook her head. "No, I was just thinking about something."

Aunt Becky poured some milk for Nicky. "Thinking pretty hard," she said.

"I have to write an article tonight and I'm not sure how to deal with it," Stephanie admitted.

"Oh, that article about the Big Cleanup Week," Danny said. "I remember you telling me about it. I'm so glad you're involved with that, Steph. It's important to participate in things that will help your school."

Stephanie just nodded. If her father only knew how totally *disinterested* she was in the Big Cleanup Week . . .

"Can I be excused to go work on it?" she asked.

"You've hardly eaten anything," Danny objected. He eyed her plate with concern.

"I'm just not hungry."

"All right," he gave in reluctantly. "Joey said your stomach was bothering you this morning."

Stephanie cleared her plate from the table and hurried up to her room. Halfway up the stairs, she had an idea. Turning back, she ran into the living room.

Quickly, she gathered the magazines from the coffee and end tables. If she skimmed the magazine articles, she could probably pick up some ideas on how to make her story sound more professional. Just to be sure, she also grabbed a few hardcover books from a shelf. Now Stephanie felt more confident. Armed with the magazines and books, she'd piece together a story that would blow Eric away.

In her room, she turned on the computer and opened the file where she'd saved her article. She reread her opening paragraph. She still thought it was a catchy beginning. She'd keep what she had so far. Now she just had to add some statistics and facts. Stephanie ran through her paragraph again. This time she deleted the word "many" and substituted "twenty-five percent."

She kept making changes. When she was finished, her sentences read: *Twenty-five percent of all students interviewed use the word "lost" to describe their freshman experience. Sixty percent use the word "confused," and eighty percent use the word "nervous."*

The percentages were just guesses, but they sounded professional to Stephanie. Besides, who would ever check on her facts? she thought. No one.

She left the computer and began spreading out magazines on the floor. She read through them quickly, underlining catchy phrases such as "The perpetrator was apprehended at dawn" and "Irate citizens crowded the lobby."

Stephanie wasn't quite sure how she was going to use these words, but she wanted to have them handy, just in case she saw a place for them.

By the time Michelle came in to go to bed, Stephanie was combing through the hardcover classics she'd taken from the shelf.

"Listen to this, Michelle," she said excitedly. She read from *A Tale of Two Cities* by Charles Dickens. " 'It was the best of times. It was the worst of times . . .' Isn't that a great way to start a novel?"

"It's a little confusing, if you ask me," Michelle said.

"What do you mean?"

"Which is it?" Michelle wanted to know. "The best or the worst of times?"

"It was both," Stephanie answered.

Michelle shrugged. "Well, I think the writer should have made up his mind before he started writing the book. That sounds totally wishy-washy."

Stephanie rolled her eyes. Michelle acted like such a child sometimes. She was simply too young to understand the complexities of life.

"Oh, just go to sleep," Stephanie muttered.

"I'd like to," Michelle replied. "When are you going to be finished with your article?"

"Just ignore me," Stephanie said.

Michelle folded her arms across her chest. "I wouldn't mind doing that, but I need to turn off the light."

"Can't you sleep with the light on?"

"No."

Stephanie sighed and turned off the lamp between their beds. She left on the desk light next to her computer. "How's that?" she asked.

"I don't know," Michelle said. "I'll try." She put on her nightgown and got under the covers. Stephanie went back to her reading.

Half an hour later, Stephanie heard Michelle grumble again.

"This isn't working," she complained from beneath her covers. "I'm not sleeping yet."

"Keep trying," Stephanie told her.

Soon she heard gentle snores coming from beneath Michelle's covers. Michelle had finally fallen asleep. Stephanie checked the clock and saw that it was after eleven. She'd better start writing or she'd be up all night.

Returning to the computer, she began to type.

It was the best of freshman years. It was the worst of freshman years. Irate students crowded the lobby of the college. The cinch prof had been apprehended at dawn that morning. Everyone wanted to be in his class. . . .

The first gray-blue shards of dawn light were making their way into the room when Stephanie finally hit the print button on her screen. She never even heard the printer spitting out the finished article. Her head on her desk, she was sound asleep.

"Stephanie! Stephanie!" a voice was saying.

Stephanie lifted her head sleepily. "Of course I'll marry you, Eric," she mumbled. As she dropped her head back down on the desk, she felt a persistent shaking. What is that? she wondered. Were they having an earthquake?

"WAKE UP, STEPHANIE!" This time the voice yelled right in her ear.

Stephanie shot upright. "Wh-what?" she stammered, looking around. "What's going on?"

"School. Remember?" Michelle said. "It's a school day, and you slept right through the alarm clock."

"Right. School. Right."

Still groggy, Stephanie stumbled around the room. "I have to get dressed."

"You *are* dressed," Michelle pointed out. Stephanie turned to the mirror. She was still in her clothes from the night before. She rubbed her red-rimmed eyes. "I have to change."

She washed up in the bathroom. Then she changed into fresh jeans and a striped sweater. It was casual but sophisticated, she decided. Yesterday she'd seen one of the students on campus wearing a sweater just like it.

Stephanie was brushing out her hair, when she remembered the pages of her article lying in the printer's output tray. She smiled to herself. She'd done it! Now all she had to do was go over to the campus after school and hand it to Eric.

All that morning Stephanie walked around school in a daze. She could barely keep her eyes open.

By lunchtime she was so exhausted, she went to the nurse's office and asked to take a nap. The nurse took one look at her and let her use one of the cots. Stephanie congratulated herself for this idea. Not only did she get some sleep, but she managed to avoid seeing her friends in the cafeteria. One part of her wanted to talk to them, but another part wasn't ready yet. Maybe, once she got more sleep, she'd try to sort things out.

At the end of the day, Stephanie was gathering her things to take to the college, when Sue Kramer appeared at her locker.

Sue looked annoyed. "You were supposed to turn in your article yesterday," she said.

Stephanie stared at her until the words regis-

tered. She'd been so engrossed in the college article, she'd forgotten all about the one for *The Scribe*.

Flustered, Stephanie fumbled in her English
folder and finally pulled out the one rumpled page.
"Sorry," she said.

"That's it?" Sue stared at the paper and blinked
in surprise. "That's *all* you wrote? But, Stephanie,
you're the best writer on the paper. I saved five
columns for your article."

Stephanie shrugged. "There wasn't much to
say," she murmured.

Sue seemed stunned, but Stephanie had to get
to campus. "Got to go. Bye," she said, shutting her
locker. She hurried away, trying not to think about
the shocked look on Sue's face.

Once again Stephanie took the bus that stopped
at the campus. This time she got off and headed
straight for the newspaper office inside the Student
Center. It made her proud to realize that she was
beginning to know her way around—just like a
real college student.

She made her way through the busy lobby of
the Student Center and up the stairs. She couldn't
wait until Eric saw her article. He'd be so
impressed!

Her pace quickened as she stepped into the quiet

hallway leading to the newspaper office. She could see the door to the office was open. *Perfect!* Stephanie thought. Eric's there. Breaking into a run, she arrived in the doorway, breathless and smiling.

But something was wrong. Very wrong. Eric was there, all right, but he wasn't alone. He was with a girl. A beautiful girl with long, dark hair. And he was kissing her!

CHAPTER
14

◆ ◂ ◗ ◆

Stephanie couldn't move. She couldn't believe what she was seeing. Eric was kissing someone else. Stephanie's entire body was frozen with shock. She couldn't move—not even when the two of them slowly untangled from their passionate embrace.

This can't be real, Stephanie told herself. *This is like a scene from a movie—not from my life.*

As the couple turned to her, Stephanie realized that the girl was Sara—the same Sara who'd invited her to the dorm party.

"Hey, Stephanie!" Eric said as if nothing were wrong.

Speechless, Stephanie backed out of the door-

114

way. She couldn't even manage a hello. Without her noticing, the article she'd written slipped from her fingers and sailed slowly toward the floor.

Eric stepped toward her. "Stephanie, what's wrong?"

Stephanie whirled away from him and ran down the hall.

"You dropped something!" Eric called, racing after her.

Stephanie kept running—until she felt Eric's hand close over her arm.

"What's the matter, Steph?" he asked anxiously. "Why are you running away?"

Stephanie stopped, but she couldn't turn around to face him. Instead, she just stared at the floor.

What an idiot she'd been! She'd acted like a fool. She sniffed, trying to stop the tears from streaming down her cheeks.

With one hand on her shoulder, Eric turned her around. "Tell me what's wrong," he pleaded.

He didn't have a clue, she realized. He didn't have the slightest idea that she would be upset by the sight of him kissing Sara.

"Stephanie," he said. "What is it?"

"I thought you liked me," she blurted out.

"I do like you," Eric said. "I—" And then he understood. "Oh, you mean . . ."

Stephanie nodded.

"Didn't you know about Sara and me?" he asked gently. "We've been going together for over a year. It seems like everyone knows we're a couple."

"*I* didn't," Stephanie murmured.

Eric nodded. "I forgot that you're a transfer student," he said. There was an uncomfortable moment as they stared at each another. "Hey, well, let me read this article," Eric said, holding up Stephanie's story. "I bet it's terrific."

But as Eric read the article, the smile on his face gradually faded. He frowned and a deep line appeared across his forehead. Stephanie felt herself grow cold inside. What was wrong? Eric flipped the page and his mouth tightened.

"You hate it," she said, guessing from the look on his face.

He put the paper down and sighed uncomfortably. He shifted from foot to foot. "It's, um . . . not exactly what I had in mind."

Stephanie couldn't understand it. She thought she'd given him *exactly* what he'd wanted.

"What do you mean?" Stephanie took the papers from him and began to read aloud. "My high school days were now gone with the wind, wiped clean by the sands of time." She looked back at him. "You didn't like that?"

116

"It's too . . . melodramatic," Eric explained. "And where did you find those percentages in the beginning?" he went on. "Twenty-five percent, sixty percent, and eighty percent—that adds up to a hundred sixty-five percent of the students! Those numbers don't make any sense."

"I made them up," she admitted sheepishly.

"I had a feeling," he said. "You made up the rest of it, too. Didn't you?"

Stephanie nodded. She wished the floor would open up and swallow her.

"Look, Stephanie." Eric's voice softened. He didn't sound as angry now. "Maybe this assignment was too hard for someone who hasn't even completed freshman English and—"

"Freshman English!" Stephanie blurted out. "I haven't even finished ninth-grade English!"

"What?" Eric demanded.

Stephanie clapped a hand over her mouth. She couldn't believe she'd actually said that. She'd given away her secret.

"I—I mean, I haven't even finished ninth-level freshman English," she said quickly.

"What are you talking about?" Eric asked. "There's no such thing as ninth-level freshman English!"

Stephanie knew she couldn't keep it up. She had

to tell him the truth. She stared down at the floor. "I'm not a college student," she said in a small voice.

"You're in high school?" Eric gasped.

Still not looking at him, she shook her head. This was so embarrassing! In fact, it was more than embarrassing—it was the worst moment of her whole life.

"You're not even in high school?" His voice sounded choked.

Cringing, Stephanie nodded. "Middle school," she whispered.

The long silence that followed forced Stephanie to look up to see what Eric was doing. He was reading her article again.

"Of course," he said. He started to smile. "This sounds exactly like a kid trying to sound like a college student. Exactly." He put down the article and burst into laughter. "That's a good one," he chuckled. "What a goof! You really fooled me, Stephanie! I thought you were a freshman!"

Stephanie snatched the article from his hands. "I have to go," she managed to say. Then she spun around and stumbled blindly through the throng of students in the center.

For the first time, Stephanie felt completely out of place on the campus. Everyone seemed to be staring at her as if they, too, had suddenly discovered that she was only a ninth-grader *pretending* to be in college.

Oh, no! she thought. A security guard in a gray uniform was striding toward her. He knows I'm a fake, too! Stephanie thought frantically. He's going to throw me out!

That would be the final, total humiliation. Stephanie couldn't let it happen. She darted through the crowd of students toward the front door. And as she did she bumped right into a girl with short blond hair. The girl's books sailed out of her arms and scattered all over the walkway.

"Stephanie!" she exclaimed.

Stephanie stiffened as she locked eyes with her older sister.

"You are in major trouble now," D.J. said in an ominous voice.

CHAPTER
15

◆ ◀ ▸ ◆

The moment Stephanie saw D.J., her self-control disappeared. Leaning against her sister, she began to sob uncontrollably.

"What is it? What happened?" D.J. asked. Her angry expression softened. Now she just looked worried. "What's wrong, Steph?"

"I thought he liked me," Stephanie wailed. "But he doesn't. He likes Sara."

D.J. put her arm around Stephanie and let her cry for a few more minutes. "Let's go to the coffee house," she suggested gently. "I'll buy you a cup of tea or something."

Stephanie was thankful that D.J. wasn't giving her a hard time about being there. At that moment she couldn't have listened to it, not with everything else that had already gone wrong.

Still sniffling, Stephanie let D.J. lead her to a little glass table in the cafe.

"You look exhausted," D.J. commented when she returned with two cups of hot tea and two doughnuts. "Michelle told me you were up all night."

Stephanie nodded as she bit into the doughnut. It tasted delicious. Suddenly, she remembered she hadn't eaten anything since breakfast.

Stephanie told D.J. everything about what had happened with Eric—how he'd hated the article, and how he'd been kissing Sara Bendix.

She expected D.J. to say "I told you so." In fact, Stephanie wouldn't have even blamed her if she did. But all D.J. did was listen sympathetically.

"Poor Stephanie," D.J. murmured. "You've been through a lot."

"Tell me about it," Stephanie agreed, her eyes welling with tears all over again.

D.J. handed Stephanie a napkin. "You know, Steph, I loved middle school," she said. "It was a fun time for me. I don't know why you're in such a hurry to be done with it. Some days I wish I were still there."

"You do?" Stephanie couldn't believe it.

"Absolutely," D.J. said. "The work is easier. And there's less of it. You have time for after-school activities. Your friends are all there. I have friends in college, but it's not the same. This school is so huge. Back in middle school and high school everyone knew me. I was totally comfortable. Here I sometimes feel a little lost."

"But you like college, don't you?" Stephanie asked.

"I love it. Still, I can't imagine starting college after ninth grade. It's the kind of experience you have to build up to slowly."

Stephanie nodded. Her sister was making sense. "I suppose I should at least try high school first," she mumbled.

D.J. smiled. "Definitely."

Propping her chin in her hands, Stephanie stared down into her tea. "I was so sure that Eric liked me, though. Just the other day he bought me a soda."

"He probably does like you—as a person—but he already has a girlfriend."

"Don't remind me," Stephanie groaned.

D.J. patted her arm. "You'll meet other guys who are just as nice."

"Not as nice as Eric," Stephanie said. "Even if he is a little old for me."

"Well, who knows?" D.J. shrugged. "If it was really meant to be, maybe someday the two of you will work together on a newspaper somewhere, while Sara—"

"Joins the space program and is living on the moon," Stephanie put in hopefully. The two of them burst out laughing.

"It could happen, you know," Stephanie said. As far-fetched as the idea was, somehow it cheered her up.

A moment later, D.J. stood up. "I have to get to class," she said, glancing at her watch. "My classroom is close to the bus stop, though. Want to walk over together?"

"Sure," Stephanie agreed.

It was fun to walk across campus with D.J. Having her big sister by her side made Stephanie feel safe—and not so lonely.

When they reached the bus stop, she hugged D.J. "Thanks," she said.

"No problem," D.J. replied, hugging her back. "Now," she said, imitating a parent's tone. "Go home—and act your age!"

"I will," Stephanie promised.

On the ride home, Stephanie thought hard about everything that had happened since last Friday. One thing was for sure—she had to make things right again with Darcy and Allie. She was embarrassed at what a jerk she'd been.

Stephanie headed straight for Allie's house when she got off the bus. Part of her hoped Allie and Darcy would be there. Another part of her hoped they wouldn't. This wasn't going to be easy.

Allie's mother answered the door. "Hi Stephanie," Mrs. Taylor said. "Allie and Darcy are upstairs working on a skit they're going to perform at a school assembly." She smiled. "It sounds pretty funny."

"Thanks, Mrs. Taylor," Stephanie said. She swallowed hard before starting up the stairs.

Stephanie could hear laughter coming from Allie's bedroom. She winced. It hurt a little to know that her best friends were having so much fun without her.

Stephanie hesitated on the landing. From where she was standing, she could see into the room through Allie's open door.

"Yuck! This school is a mess!" Darcy said, reciting the lines from the skit. "What a dump!"

Holding a pretend magic wand, Allie hurried toward her. "I'm the Clean-up Fairy," she said in a squeaky voice. "I'll help you fix this wreck in a jiffy."

"Oh, who needs you, Miss Fairy Sunshine!" Darcy growled. As she spoke those crabby lines, both Darcy and Allie cracked up.

"This is so stupid, it's funny!" Allie cried. She was laughing so hard, she was holding her stomach.

"Wait till everyone else sees this dumb skit." Darcy giggled. "We'll never hear the end of it."

Their laughter was so contagious that Stephanie started laughing, too.

Her friends whirled toward the doorway at the same time. "What are you doing here?" Darcy asked, frowning.

"Why aren't you over at campus with your sophisticated college friends?" Allie chimed in.

"Because I'd rather be here," Stephanie told them honestly.

"Since when?" Darcy snapped.

Stephanie drew in a breath. "Since I discovered I'm not as *mature* as I thought."

Darcy and Allie looked surprised.

"I thought *we* were the immature ones," Darcy said. Stephanie smiled slyly. "You are," she said. "You're both way immature. But that's why I like you. We're three of a kind."

Darcy and Allie glanced at one another. Stephanie

could tell they were trying to decide if they should forgive her.

"Look, guys," she said quickly. "I'm so sorry. I've been a major jerk. I'm really, really, really, sorry—okay? You guys aren't the least bit immature, not compared to me."

Allie scooped up a pair of balled-up socks on her dresser and chucked them at Stephanie. "How's that for immature?" she said as the socks bounced off Stephanie's shoulder.

Stephanie caught them and tossed them back at her. "Perfect," she said, laughing. She stepped into the room. "Can I have my old part in the skit back?"

There was a brief silence. Then Darcy spoke up. "We crossed out all your lines and rewrote the skit, but I still have a copy of the first script we wrote," she said. "We can go back to that one." Then Darcy smiled at her. "It's good to have you back, Steph."

"Thanks," Stephanie said.

For the rest of the afternoon, they rehearsed the skit. All Stephanie could think about was how funny the skit was—and about how she hadn't laughed this hard for a long time.

Around supper time, she finally arrived home. Michelle was the first to greet her. "Someone named Sue Kramer called," she reported, reading a message from the note pad by the phone. "She said she can't take your article the way it is. Should she put something different in that space or do you want to work on it some more tonight?"

Stephanie thanked her sister and picked up the phone to call Sue. "Sorry about the article," she said when Sue came on. "I know it was crummy. I'll write you a new one by tomorrow."

Then she went to her room and began working on it. *"John Muir Middle School is a great place,"* she typed, *"but it needs a little help. Luckily, it has terrific students who know exactly what to do. . . ."*

She smiled as she typed. It felt wonderful to be her old, middle-school self again. But, still, she couldn't help thinking about her college article. It bothered her that Eric had laughed at it. For some reason, she wanted to show him that she *was* really a good writer. How could she do that though? Somehow, she had to find a way.

CHAPTER
16

◆ ◂ ▸ ◆

"Hey, look! *The Scribe* is out!" Darcy exclaimed.

Stephanie glanced toward the cafeteria. A cardboard box filled with copies of the school paper had just been placed outside the doors.

Stephanie got there first and grabbed a copy. "My story's on the front page!" she cried. After her experience as a "college" reporter, she hadn't been feeling all that confident about her writing. But Sue Kramer had liked her follow-up article about the Big Cleanup Week enough to put it on the front page, where the strongest stories always appeared.

Even though she knew what it said, Stephanie read the article through again. It *was* good—clear and interesting. Much better than what she'd written for Eric.

Maybe that's because this time I knew what I was talking about, she mused.

Mr. Merlin, the media skills teacher, walked by. "Nice article, Steph," he said. "It's good to see you display a little more enthusiasm for the Big Cleanup Week. What happened last week?"

Stephanie shook her head. "It's sort of a long story."

"A long, *strange* story," Darcy put in.

"Does it have anything to do with your idea for a sleep-over painting party?" Mr. Merlin asked.

"You heard about my idea, too?" Stephanie asked.

"Everyone in the faculty lounge heard about your idea," Mr. Merlin replied.

Stephanie groaned. "Oh, no."

"I actually thought it was a terrific idea, and that you were right. The activities should be more fun," Mr. Merlin said.

"Really?" Stephanie said.

Mr. Merlin nodded. Then he shrugged. "But I couldn't convince Mr. Thomas. Maybe next year," he added.

"He's nice," Allie whispered, and Stephanie

nodded her agreement as the teacher disappeared into the cafeteria.

"Look," Darcy said, pointing to the paper. "Here's a review of last Friday's assembly." The girls quickly skimmed the article for any mention of their skit.

"There we are," Allie said. "It says we were ridiculous but hysterical."

"Where?" Stephanie asked eagerly.

Darcy pointed to the line. "Most ridiculous of all was Stephanie Tanner in the part of the Trash Monster," she read. "Her zany humor cracked up the entire audience. What a nut!"

Stephanie grinned. It felt good to be able to act silly and ridiculous—and not to have to worry about being *mature*. "I think I'll send Eric a copy of this paper," she said.

"Why?" Darcy asked.

"I don't know." Stephanie shrugged. "Somehow I feel like I should let him see the real me."

"The nut?" Allie teased. "It sounds like he already knows you're a nut."

"You're probably right," Stephanie said. She still felt embarrassed about the whole thing. But Eric and her campus experience were both beginning to seem very far away—more like a dream than something that had actually happened.

She glanced up as a cute boy with long dark hair walked past them on his way into the lunchroom.

Darcy gripped Stephanie's wrist. "Who's he?"

"I don't know. He must be new," Allie replied.

"Come on," Stephanie said. "Let's go meet him."

She grabbed Allie and Darcy and dragged them toward the cafeteria. She knew that chasing down the new boy was almost as silly and immature as playing the Trash Monster in last Friday's skit.

But it's lots of fun, Stephanie thought. *I love being in the ninth grade!*

FULL HOUSE™
Michelle

#5: THE GHOST IN MY CLOSET 53573-0/$3.99

#6: BALLET SURPRISE 53574-9/$3.99

#7: MAJOR LEAGUE TROUBLE 53575-7/$3.99

#8: MY FOURTH-GRADE MESS 53576-5/$3.99

#9: BUNK 3, TEDDY, AND ME 56834-5/$3.99

#10: MY BEST FRIEND IS A MOVIE STAR!
(Super Edition) 56835-3/$3.99

#11: THE BIG TURKEY ESCAPE 56836-1/$3.99

#12: THE SUBSTITUTE TEACHER 00364-X/$3.99

#13: CALLING ALL PLANETS 00365-8/$3.99

#14: I'VE GOT A SECRET 00366-6/$3.99

#15: HOW TO BE COOL 00833-1/$3.99

#16: THE NOT-SO-GREAT OUTDOORS 00835-8/$3.99

#17: MY HO-HO-HORRIBLE CHRISTMAS 00836-6/$3.99

MY AWESOME HOLIDAY FRIENDSHIP BOOK
(An Activity Book) 00840-4/$3.99

FULL HOUSE MICHELLE OMNIBUS 02181-8/$6.99

A MINSTREL® BOOK

Published by Pocket Books

Simon & Schuster Mail Order Dept. BWB
200 Old Tappan Rd., Old Tappan, N.J. 07675

Please send me the books I have checked above. I am enclosing $_____ (please add $0.75 to cover the postage and handling for each order. Please add appropriate sales tax). Send check or money order--no cash or C.O.D.'s please. Allow up to six weeks for delivery. For purchase over $10.00 you may use VISA: card number, expiration date and customer signature must be included.

Name _____

Address _____

City _____ State/Zip _____

VISA Card # _____ Exp.Date _____

Signature _____

1033-24

FULL HOUSE
Stephanie™

Title	Order Info
PHONE CALL FROM A FLAMINGO	88004-7/$3.99
THE BOY-OH-BOY NEXT DOOR	88121-3/$3.99
TWIN TROUBLES	88290-2/$3.99
HIP HOP TILL YOU DROP	88291-0/$3.99
HERE COMES THE BRAND NEW ME	89858-2/$3.99
THE SECRET'S OUT	89859-0/$3.99
DADDY'S NOT-SO-LITTLE GIRL	89860-4/$3.99
P.S. FRIENDS FOREVER	89861-2/$3.99
GETTING EVEN WITH THE FLAMINGOES	52273-6/$3.99
THE DUDE OF MY DREAMS	52274-4/$3.99
BACK-TO-SCHOOL COOL	52275-2/$3.99
PICTURE ME FAMOUS	52276-0/$3.99
TWO-FOR-ONE CHRISTMAS FUN	53546-3/$3.99
THE BIG FIX-UP MIX-UP	53547-1/$3.99
TEN WAYS TO WRECK A DATE	53548-X/$3.99
WISH UPON A VCR	53549-8/$3.99
DOUBLES OR NOTHING	56841-8/$3.99
SUGAR AND SPICE ADVICE	56842-6/$3.99
NEVER TRUST A FLAMINGO	56843-4/$3.99
THE TRUTH ABOUT BOYS	00361-5/$3.99
CRAZY ABOUT THE FUTURE	00362-3/$3.99
MY SECRET ADMIRER	00363-1/$3.99
BLUE RIBBON CHRISTMAS	00830-7/$3.99
THE STORY ON OLDER BOYS	00831-5/$3.99

It doesn't matter if you live around the corner...
or around the world...
If you are a fan of Mary-Kate and Ashley Olsen,
you should be a member of

MARY-KATE + ASHLEY'S FUN CLUB™

Here's what you get:
Our Funzine™
An autographed color photo
Two black & white individual photos
A full size color poster
An official **Fun Club**™ membership card
A **Fun Club**™ school folder
Two special **Fun Club**™ surprises
A holiday card
Fun Club™ collectibles catalog
Plus a **Fun Club**™ box to keep everything in

To join Mary-Kate + Ashley's Fun Club™, fill out the form
below and send it along with

U.S. Residents – $17.00
Canadian Residents – $22 U.S. Funds
International Residents – $27 U.S. Funds

MARY-KATE + ASHLEY'S FUN CLUB™
859 HOLLYWOOD WAY, SUITE 275
BURBANK, CA 91505

NAME:_____

ADDRESS:_____

_CITY:_____ STATE:_____ ZIP:_____

PHONE:(___) _____ BIRTHDATE:_____

1242